Critical acclaim for

Melissa Senate

Love You to Death
"Readers will cheer Abby every step of the way as
she tries to clear her name and find her prince for
whom the glass slipper will finally fit."
—*Publishers Weekly*

"Will leave readers shaking their heads laughing."
—*Romantic Times*

The Breakup Club
"Senate's latest has her trademark quirky pacing and
sympathetic, lovable characters, proving once again
she's one of Red Dress Ink's brightest talents."
—*Booklist*

"One of the many gifts Senate brings
to the writing table is her ability to establish
equally compelling stories for four fascinating
characters. That she does so with humor and insight
adds to the pleasures of the novel."
—*Romantic Times*

Whose Wedding is it Anyway?
"[Senate] wittily debunks the idea
of a perfect wedding."
—*Marie Claire*

"Unexpected twists in the story distinguish Senate's
novel from the pack of bride-to-be books."
—*Booklist*

Melissa Senate

Questions to Ask Before Marrying

RED
DRESS
I N K
TM

First edition June 2008

QUESTIONS TO ASK BEFORE MARRYING

A Red Dress Ink novel

ISBN-13: 978-0-373-89560-1
ISBN-10:   0-373-89560-7

www.RedDressInk.com

Printed in U.S.A.

Acknowledgment

The year I wrote this book (my editor might correct that to year *and a half*) was a funny year. Funny strange and funny ha-ha. I have to say a huge thanks to many for their support, good cheer, kindness, patience and inspiration, starting with said editor, Linda McFall, Margaret O'Neill Marbury, Joan Marlow Golan, Selina McLemore and Melissa Caraway (world's most organized person).

To my agent, Kim Witherspoon, and the dynamo Alexis Hurley.

To my family, for their constant support through thick and thin.

To my friends Elizabeth Zurkan and Lee Naftali and Karen Hirsch for listening (endlessly).

To Lee Nichols (she gets two categories), Kristin Harmel, Sarah Mylnowski, Alison Pace, and Lynda Curnyn for their brilliant advice.

A very special thanks to the staff at Books, Etc. in Falmouth, Maine, for their continued and very cheerful support of a local author.

To Adam, who is a friend indeed.

And to my precious Max, who inspires me to be better at everything.

This book is dedicated to Karen Hirsch,
for twenty-five(!) years of friendship

1

ACCORDING TO AN OFTEN-REFERENCED *NEW YORK TIMES* ARTICLE, there are fifteen questions you should ask yourself and The One before marrying. About children (how many... who will be primary caretaker?), finances (spender...saver?), sex (how often...you're not secretly gay are you?), in-laws (get the rules in writing!), and even if there should be a television in the bedroom. But the most important question, the one that had me second-guessing my near instantaneous acceptance of Tom's marriage proposal, was the last. Number fifteen. About the strength of the relationship and whether it would withstand challenges.

Such as my twin sister, Stella.

"This is an intervention," Stella said, stretching her skinny arms across my bedroom doorway to block my escape into the living room, where my engagement party was in full swing. "From a marriage that will bore you to death before your first anniversary."

She wasn't laughing. Shouldn't there be a laugh after a comment like that? A *just kidding?*

"Run for your life, Ruby," she whispered. "You don't want to die before your thirtieth birthday, do you?" She added the trademark head tilt she'd affected by studying Angelina Jolie.

Stella and I were not identical twins. Clearly. We had little in common other than the first half of our childhoods, our big-toothed smiles and our taste in men—until now, until Tom.

She objected to his looks, which she described as classic woodwork. She objected to his clothes, which she described as nerdometer-blowing. She objected to his dinner conversation, which she described as better than Sominex.

My response: *You and I are not the same person, Stella. We never have been.* Even if we used to be attracted to the same type of man, starting with three-foot four-inch tall Danny Peel in preschool.

Tom was the man for me. Granted, I was a bit stumped on some of the questions from the *New York Times* article. But wasn't *compromise* a good answer—the right answer— to many of them? For example, to Tom wanting *four* kids, like his parents had, like both his sisters had (his brother wasn't yet married). We would agree on two. Though he really, really, really wanted four. And as a twin, I really,

really, really liked the idea of having just one child, lavishing all my attention on him or her. When I mentioned that, Tom had looked at me as though I had four heads, and said there was plenty of time to figure all that out.

Yeah, to convince you to pop out four, Stella had commented when I'd mistakenly been thinking out loud last Thanksgiving. Tom and I had been talking about our future even then. *After the first kid, he'll make you feel guilty about not giving Bore Jr. a sibling, so you'll get knocked up again, with twins because they run in the family. Then he'll make you feel guilty about Bore Jr. being the only non-twin, and you'll be pregnant again. Suddenly, you have four, just like he wanted. And right, you'll co-parent.* She'd cracked up for a good half minute.

At least Tom and I were both savers, so that was good for the finance question, even if Tom did go overboard in the supermarket, consistently choosing, say, generic toilet paper over Quilted Northern, which I felt was worth the extra money. *Not only is he a cheapskate,* Stella had said, *but he does it so you won't ask him to go grocery shopping in the first place. You say he's not a typical guy, Rubes, but trust me, that is a typical guy.*

And Tom did like a television in the bedroom, tuned to either CNN or a Red Sox game. I wasn't so crazy about that. But it was hardly a deal breaker.

Then there was sex. Our sex life could be described like that hilarious split screen scene in *Annie Hall,* when both Annie and Alvy are separately at their therapists' offices and when asked how often they have sex, Annie says: "Constantly. I'd say three times a week." And Alvy says, "Hardly ever. Maybe *three* times a week." This, I hadn't shared with my sister. I didn't have to, since Stella often said that "the sex must suck." It didn't, not really.

It wasn't that I *wasn't* attracted to Tom because I was, to a degree. He was tall, lankily muscular, with washboard abs and he smelled good, like Ivory soap. And he was perfectly attractive in a bit of a bland way. He was also great company, kind, intelligent, often funny, responsible and solid as the ole rock. But—

"Let me guess," Stella continued, dropping her arms to twirl a strand of her long, dark hair around her finger. "Mr. Personality proposed at school. In front of seventh graders."

I didn't know why I laughed. It wasn't funny. Stella assuming such a thing—or the fact that she was right.

"And you said *yes,*" she whispered. "Yes to being *Ruby Truby.*" She rolled her eyes and shook her head. "Ruby Truby," she repeated, then turned and disappeared into the crowd in the living room, settling herself in a chair next to our great-grandmother, Zelda, our only other relative in the world, unless you counted our father and his extended family, which you couldn't.

I could barely count Stella.

I glanced around for Tom; he was on the deck, wearing his engagement gift from one of his young nieces, a white apron embroidered with *I Rock As An Uncle* and splattered with preschool-made painted handprints. He was brushing barbecue sauce on the chicken while chatting with a bunch of his male relatives, who were tall and lanky like him.

Just over a week ago on the last day of school, Tom Truby, in the durable Dockers and trademark sweater-vest that drove Stella nuts, knocked on my classroom door during study hall for "A moment, Ms. Miller?" There had been the usual whistles and "You go, Truby!" from the students, my eighth-grade English class. Teacher romances weren't common at Blueberry Hills Academy.

I decided not to confirm to Stella that Tom *had* proposed in school. In the stairwell. During fourth period. But on one knee, at least.

The stairs were sort of romantic. Tom and I had met on those steps on my first day at BLA (affectionately acronymed with a silent *H* by students and faculty alike) two and a half years ago. I'd been going up; he'd been going down, but then he'd suddenly jogged up backward to my step and stared at me for half a second before extending his hand with a friendly, "Tom Truby, AP English and European History." My first thought was *nerdy*. My second was *but kinda hot underneath that navy-blue sweater-vest.* My third was *I like the way he's looking at me with those intelligent blue eyes.* Which, for that one unguarded moment, was passionately.

The English Chair, Meg Fitzmaurice, had come down the stairs then. She'd clapped her arm around me and said, "Welcome to the loony bin, Ruby. I see you've already met Tom Truby." (Who had since continued back down.) "If you need anything, he's your guy. True as his name." Then she leaned in and whispered, "But avoid Nick McDermott. You'll know why when you meet him, but I'll give you a hint. The entire female faculty refers to him as Mr. McDreamy. You know, like from *Grey's Anatomy.*"

Two and a half years later, if the sight of Mr. McDreamy could still manage to make the air whoosh out of my body at my own engagement party, I would accept that *I,* myself, was a challenge to my future with Tom, to our marriage. I would accept that Stella (who knew nothing of my feelings for Nick) was right, that I did require an intervention. Because it was one thing to marry a man you did love— but maybe, if you were very honest with yourself, more like a friend than anything—a man who would make a trustworthy, dependable husband, a wonderful, doting father. But it was another to do so knowing that you were in love with someone else, someone you couldn't have the way you would want. Or need.

What you wanted, what you needed, you had said yes to, and for good reason. You were an intelligent woman. You overthought, in fact. Something you'd been accused of since kindergarten. But you didn't have to overthink what you craved, what you fantasized about, what stopped you from all rational thought several times a day, which now stood on the deck of your home, a guest at your engagement party.

Nick, of course, had spent a good fifteen minutes charming my great-grandmother, who'd uttered, "My, is he *handsome!*" three times already. But charming women of all ages was Nick's specialty. Including twelve- to eighteen-year-old girls, his students, into passionate discussions and essays about *The Merchant of Venice* and *To Kill a Mockingbird*. The part of Nick that stole the breath out of me was ninety-nine percent (okay, seventy-five percent) *that:* the maverick teacher who could command a classroom of adolescents at their hormoniest worst and transfix them by relating centuries-old relationships to their own. He managed to make voice-cracking thirteen-year-old boys feel so much for *Henry V* that they broke out into soliloquies in the cafeteria, their French fries raised as swords, ketchup splattered on their T-shirts as they fell in bloody battle.

Yes, he was gorgeous. In that almost movie-star way. Thirty-four. Six-one. Lankily muscular. Two dimples. Sparkling dark-brown eyes and thick, dark-brown sexy hair. Fair, fair skin that somehow managed to tan even before the last day of school. That perfect Roman nose—broken once in a fight with someone's husband. He also came complete with a small trust fund that enabled him to live in a gorgeous, historic apartment in Portland's West End, drive a silver Porsche and do exactly what he wanted with his life, which was to teach.

As I headed out onto the deck I ignored Stella, who was French braiding the hair of one of Tom's little nieces. The deck was crowded with Trubys, faculty from BLA and friends. Tom, adding the vegetable shish kebabs to the grill, was deep in conversation with his male relatives about the

Red Sox and whether they'd make it to the play-offs. Nick stood alone by the railing, staring out at the view of downtown Blueberry Hills, the town square and the BLA campus just across the street.

Blueberry Hills was your typical Maine coastal town: lovely and quaint, five white clapboard churches with their magnificent steeples lining the mile-long Main Street, the yellow Victorians (mine was a miniature yellow Victorian) and white antique farmhouses, the swing sets in backyards full of children, the joggers, the baby strollers, the dogs, the majestic trees. Maine in June was at its most glorious. Temperatures, like today, in the low seventies, brilliant sunshine.

"Your mother would be so proud," Grammy Zelda said as she and her boyfriend, Harold, who lived next door to each other at the Blueberry Hills nursing home (she insisted on living there for her "independence"), shuffled toward me, plates of cake crumbs in their hands. "Tom is a real nice fella," she whispered. "Quality. She'd be so happy that you didn't end up with someone like your father." She threw up a hand in disgust, then spit on her arm. "I shouldn't even say his name. The *meshugener.*"

I eyed Nick and had to admit that he and my father, Eric Miller, shared a certain resemblance beyond the womanizing. And the charm. They were both tall, dark-haired and too handsome. They both had dimples, though my father had just one. But a difference was that Nick was here, celebrating my engagement with me. And my father, whom I hadn't seen since I was six, wasn't.

"Tom is a good man," I said to Zelda. "The best." He was. *I am an engaged woman now. Ruby Truby rhymes! Rhyme is good! I will stop ogling Nick McDermott. I will stop imagining. Wondering. Today I will officially stop.*

Not that there hadn't been chances these past two and a half years. Nick and I had become instant friends my first week at BLA. Good friends. We spent a lot of time together. And he'd made flirtatious little comments from day one. But I *knew* Nick McDermott. Knew his type, too. You had a night, maybe a great couple of weeks, with Nick McDermott. But you had a future, a lifetime, with Tom Truby.

As Zelda and Harold headed back inside, Nick gestured me over. Between grading finals and endless congratulatory lunches and dinners with faculty and various members of the Truby family, I hadn't spent much time alone with Nick during the past week. So this would be the litmus test. Would the air whoosh out of me the moment those dark, dark eyes were looking at me? Or would I finally, at my own engagement party, be immune to Mr. McDreamy?

"So you're getting married," he said. "You're off the market. I've lost my chance."

The air whooshed, as always.

He was teasing me, of course. But still, my first thought was: Have you? If you stretched your arms out on either side and said: *Ruby Miller, this is an intervention. You can't marry Tom because you will die of what-if before your first anniversary,* would I say okay? And okay to what? The one night? The just-to-finally-*know*?

"Take a walk with me?" he asked, nodding at the yard below.

We headed down the steps to the grass and followed the stone path to the side yard where Tom had built a white wooden swing for us when we moved in together last summer. It was the only place outside on our property where we had absolute privacy, and Tom and I often sat on the swing in nice weather, reading or grading exams or just talking.

Nick plucked a bluebell from my little garden, tucked my hair behind my ear and slid the stem through. "Tom's lucky," he said as he sat down on the swing.

Nick McDermott had been casually touching me, casually slinging his arm around me, casually kissing me on the cheek or pecking me on the lips for two and a half years. Yet even the lightest touch, the most casual gesture, undid me. This was bad. Wrong, too. But as our principal liked to say to every situation, *It is what it is.* And *it* didn't have to mean anything. Nick was like a movie star, a rock star, unattainable up there on the big screen, the big stage. He wasn't real. "I'm lucky, too," I said, sitting down next to him. "He's a great guy."

Nick glanced at me for a moment, then let out a short breath. "I meant what I said before, Ruby. About losing my chance. I've always thought about us, you know."

I stared at him. And he stared back.

He was serious. Dead serious. He wasn't smiling. Or laughing. Or saying, *You and me. Ha. Like that would work for five minutes.* And then laughing some more. "And I'm not talking about sex," he added. "I mean, I am. Of course. But I'm talking about the real thing. Ever since you got engaged, I can't stop thinking about you. About *us,* Ruby. About the what-if, you know?"

Whoa, whoa, whoa.

I did know. But—and the *but* kept me from flinging myself into his arms and ripping off his clothes—Nick had had sex with just about every female member of the BLA faculty, plus subs and the hot fifty-something lunch lady (she looked remarkably like Kim Basinger). Even if he was serious, I could *not* take him seriously. I hadn't from first flirt my first day at BLA. And I most certainly couldn't now, at my engagement party. I'd said yes to Tom Truby, true as his name. We were both savers!

And the strength of our bond was strong enough to withstand challenges, both big and small. I believed that.

He was staring at me with those dark, dark eyes. Waiting. For what, though? A game? *You're engaged so now I want you?* But Nick didn't play games with me. Never had. I was his *best* friend. He couldn't be my best friend because I could never tell him my biggest secret. And I wasn't about to now.

"I'd better get back to the party," I blurted out and then ran around the house and back up the steps and collided with Tom on the deck.

He gently touched the bluebell in my hair. "I was just looking for you. Stella's going through my closet and saying things like, 'Oh, God, no' and 'Did he steal this from Mr. Rogers?'"

"I'll take care of it," I said, my heart booming in my chest. "Sorry."

He smiled and kissed my hand. "I'm glad she came. You okay?"

Ha. I thought Stella was going to be the problem?

2

I SMILED MY WAY THROUGH THE CROWD ON THE DECK, DESPERATE to be alone, to think, to chant my way out of this: Tom, good. Nick, bad. Tom, good. Nick, bad. But someone grabbed my hand. It was Tom's sister, Caroline, who'd shown up at our house with a stack of bridal magazines the day after we'd gotten engaged. She was saying something now about pink satin, and how it complemented every woman's skin tone— if it was the right pink, and she knew her pinks. How many bridesmaids did I envision, she wanted to know. I vaguely realized that there were ellipses involved, that she was waiting for me to ask her to be in my bridal party. A moment later, her six-year-old daughter, Bree, ran over in hysterics because her hair wasn't long enough for a French braid like her sister was now sporting.

Pink bridesmaids are good. Tom is good. Nick is bad.

I offered her a rueful smile and slipped inside the house and headed to the bedroom, where I found Stella staring at herself in the full-length mirror attached to the closet door, checking herself out from every conceivable direction. She usually made kissy faces at herself in mirrors, pouting her lips like Anna Nicole Smith. But now she just stared at herself as though she didn't like what she saw.

I wished I could tell her what just happened on that swing, but she'd steamroll me before I had a chance to think, to process. She might even walk out into the living room, say she had an announcement and declare to everyone: *I am ending the engagement between my sister and Tom. She is in love with another man, who's here, by the way, and who has just told her that he's always thought about them! Please take back your toasters and crystal vases and go home, people!*

I tried to think, tried to process, but Stella was distracting me with her restlessness. She'd moved from the mirror to my bed, where she was now flipping through a *People* magazine she'd grabbed from my nightstand. She'd been in and out of my bedroom all afternoon, barely mingling, politely excusing herself from anyone's attempt to engage her in conversation, which was usually, *So you're Ruby's twin! You look nothing alike! You're fraternal twins, right?*

She flung aside the magazine, then went over to my dressing table and started brushing her hair with my fake brush, the antique meant for decoration. I'd always been envious of Stella's hair, which was long, dark, glossy, and straight-wavy. I'd inherited my mother's fine blond hair, which looked thin if it got too long, so it was a sort of non-length just above my shoulders. Stella opened my jewelry box and pawed through it. She fastened our mother's heart locket pendant around her neck, the delicate gold chain pretty against her tanned skin. She went back to my bed and the *People*.

"Stella…you can't keep that," I said. We'd gone through our mother's jewelry box the weekend of her funeral two years ago. Surprisingly, neither of us had reached for the same pieces. "You know how I feel about that necklace." It had been a gift to my mother from my father on one of their very early anniversaries. I would never wear it, since it hardly seemed to mean anything, but the sentiment in which it was given had meant something. Did mean something. It was that sentiment I wanted.

She didn't say anything. I realized she was staring at my engagement ring.

"Does it bother you?" I asked, glancing at the one-carat round diamond, which had also been my mother's.

She shook her head and swept her hair up into a bun, then let it cascade around her shoulders. "Whoever gets engaged first gets the ring. That was Mom's deal. But there should have been conditions, Ruby. Like marrying someone you actually love."

Whoa. Current situation aside, what did Stella know about how I felt? I hadn't seen her since early December, six months ago. And before that, Thanksgiving, but before that, it had been our birthdays last July. Stella was a flitter. She barely e-mailed, either.

"I do love Tom," I said, staring at the ring. That *was* the truth. I did love him. I just was sort of maybe in love with someone else who was now telling me, at this eleventh hour, that he *thought about us.*

"You *said* you didn't, Ruby. And you don't."

"I said I didn't two years ago. On the worst day of my life."

She shrugged and flipped another page.

What I said I'd said on the deck of my mother's house, late at night after her funeral. It had been cold for early December, barely twenty degrees, which was cold even for Maine that early in the winter. Stella and I were sitting on the wooden slats, looking out onto our mother's favorite place of all, her gardens, which in summer were ablaze with color. We were bundled up in down jackets and sipping at the harsh liquor someone poured for us, whiskey. We also had a tin of blueberries, our mother's only addiction.

Our mother, all we had in the world aside from each other and Grammy Zelda, had been in a car accident. There'd been a deer and someone stopping short on a rural highway, someone in a huge SUV. My mother's little car hadn't stood a chance behind that truck. Its driver had, though, barely. Forget the deer.

The cards from my students, still so new to me then, made me cry. The kids and their parents knocked on the door with quiches and pies, and I accepted each with half a thank-you before I burst into tears, leaving them to stand there not knowing what to say, what to do. And then Tom, who I'd been dating for only three months, would appear behind me, graciously thank the visitor, to their immense relief, and lead me into my bedroom for a good long hug.

The day of the funeral, Tom spent hours at my side, politely making small talk to strangers, mostly my mother's friends and co-workers at the library, then cleaned up the living room and kitchen of her house, Saran-wrapping casseroles and cakes and replenishing boxes of Kleenex while I sat on the deck with Stella, who I'd seen only three times that year. That was Tom Truby at three months.

What I'd said, what I'd whispered to her between the whiskey and the blueberries, my voice cracking, was: "Despite all this, I still can't work up any *love* for him. If *only* I could love him."

I'd wanted to love him then. I'd worked so hard at it since our third date, when I'd realized that Tom and I were headed for a relationship. Being with him, talking to him, was effortless. And the way he looked at me made up for my lack of passion for him. He would look at me—whether from across a romantic, candlelit table or while I was down with a cold and had a red nose and watery eyes—with true desire, which was a first for me. It always surprised me, made me feel so…sexy. Tom was easy to love.

But Stella had been throwing my words in my face ever since that night on the deck. At every occasion, few and far between—our birthdays, Thanksgiving, then the anniversary of our mother's death. No matter our cold wars or where she was at the time (one year she was living in Ireland), she came to Maine for all three. Thanksgiving was our mother's favorite holiday, and now that it was down to me and Stella and Grammy Zelda, it was written in stone that Thanksgiving would be at my house. As for our birthdays, my mother had always insisted we celebrate together, even when we were teenagers who fought even more bitterly than we did now.

And we grudgingly continued the tradition as adults, ostensibly for the sake of our mother and Grammy Zelda, who made such a fuss every year. When we lived in New York City as little kids, we always celebrated our birthdays at the famed Serendipity 3 for frozen hot chocolate. In Maine, it was a working farm that sold ice cream on an old caboose, the most incredible ice cream we'd ever had and ever would have. We'd sit in the gazebo, whether we were newly seven or newly seventeen, with Mom and Grammy Zelda, our grandmother there for a small portion of those years. And then Stella and I would go check out the bunny hut and the pigs and the billy goats, which were my favorite. There was a moratorium against fighting for those hours, difficult to stick to, but we always did manage it. I would say, *Don't you wish we could take these adorable little goats home?* And instead of telling me that the stinky goats would actually improve the smell left in our bedroom by my best friend, Liza, who was a runner, Stella would just nod.

The birthday celebrations always undid our problems until at least the next morning or next phone conversation, when we'd go back to not speaking. Stella was easy to not speak to.

The problem with me and my sister was that we seemed to understand each other's truths, but then threw that truth in the other's face without a care to the other's feelings. And the truth was the truth. I would not tell Stella that I hesitated—for just a minute in both head and heart—about saying yes to Tom. I would also not share with her that my first thought wasn't yes or no, but *Nick*. The good guy had won, the *right* guy, as he should. But somehow, based on one whiskey-induced comment two years ago, when I'd been in despair, Stella *knew*. She didn't know how I felt about Nick, though how my feelings didn't show was beyond me. But she knew I didn't love Tom the way you might love someone you were going to marry.

"Two years is a long time, Stella. Six months is a long time, too. You have no idea how I feel about *anything*. I see you a few times a year, you make some rude comments, and then you leave again."

"Whatever," she said, flipping another page. "I can stay here for a few days, right?"

Sigh. Of course she could. Because what happened when Stella came home was what always happened: I felt an incredible sense of relief, of *rightness,* despite everything, despite our differences. "You can stay in the guest room for as long as you want. But keep your comments about Tom to yourself. He proposed, I said yes, we love each other, and we're getting married." *I will not think about what Nick said. I will not put any stock into it. I'm just one of the few women in Maine who he hasn't slept with. I'm a conquest.* "If you don't want to be my maid of honor, fine."

She rolled her eyes.

"No, actually not fine," I said. "You will be my maid of honor whether you like it or not. Whether you like Tom or not. And you'll smile down the aisle. Got it?"

She finally cracked a smile. "Got it, got it. But I thought you always said you wanted to elope to Las Vegas, like Mom and Dad."

I stared at my shoes. "I don't know about that anymore." Tom wasn't really an eloper. Not with all those Trubys expecting a big wedding and pink bridesmaid dresses.

The thought of Las Vegas, with all its mystery and hard-edged glamour, the glittering lights of the strip and the strange cacti of the desert, the drive-through wedding chapels—if they really existed—had always seemed so strangely romantic to me. But mostly because our parents had eloped to Las Vegas. Because they'd been in love once. Our father had even uncharacteristically written his own vows, albeit scribbled in crayon on the back of a children's menu at Denny's, which I had now in my mother's hope chest.

Stella shut the door. "If you're going to marry Tom, despite what you said two years ago, let's drive down to Las Vegas and plan you a beautiful wedding in a nice chapel and book you a beautiful dinner reservation. And I can give you a bachelorette party the night before. And then Tom can fly down, and I'll be your witness. It'll be like our last hurrah."

I burst into tears. Stella might have been easy to not speak to, but like Tom, she was easy to love.

"Is that a yes?" she asked, handing me a tissue.

It wasn't a yes. I couldn't last thirty minutes in a car with Stella, and Las Vegas was a forty-two-hour drive. I knew this because she spent the next hour on Google Maps, printing out the driving directions (Stella had become deathly afraid of flying in the past few years). Every minute or so, she'd come find me chatting to a colleague or one of Tom's many relatives and whisper something in my ear like, "The outlaw trail where Jesse James and his gang hid would be on our route—well, it's a slight detour. I wonder if the Grand Canyon is," and then with lit-up eyes she'd disappear back to the laptop in my bedroom.

I headed there now to get away from the nonstop talk about "the wedding." About how many kids we wanted. I'd gotten so many horrified looks when I said I wanted just one child that I started saying *four,* just to get the smile so I could move on instead of having to defend myself.

Why did you have to defend your own feelings?

I shut the door behind me and took three quick deep breaths. Stella lay on her stomach on my bed, her legs crossed in the air behind her, the Google maps spread out in front of her. She pointed her pink highlighter at me. "That's going to be your life. For the next sixty years or so." She gestured at the pillows by her feet, at some envelopes lying on top. "That hot friend of yours left that for you," she added. "He said he had to go. Oh, and the Grand Canyon wouldn't be on the route. But we could take a detour if you wanted."

During one of Stella's holiday visits, "that hot friend of mine" had asked me if she was off-limits, and I said she was, and he'd respected that. If Nick and Stella had ever hooked up (to borrow a phrase from my students), I would have spontaneously combusted.

I glanced at the envelopes. One fancy, one plain, both in Nick's terrible handwriting. The fancy one was addressed to me and Tom. I opened it; it was an engagement present, a very generous gift certificate for a weekend at a famous seaside inn not far from here. The second envelope, the one addressed only to me, sort of rescinded the present. It was a note on plain paper:

Maybe we should be going there. —Nick

Deep breath. I folded the note to a tiny square and put it in my wallet.

Before I could think or process, Tom's sister found me with a "there you are!" and launched into color schemes again and how she could plan the entire wedding for us for free. Stella got up from the desk chair and whispered, "We can see the house that James Dean grew up in in Indiana!" I tried to ignore Stella, but she said, "Can I steal my sister for a minute," to Tom's sister, then pulled me into the bathroom and shut the door. "Should I call Hertz?" she asked.

Yes. Yes. Yes. Get me out of here!

No, no, no. It was crazy. And I wasn't crazy. "Stella, Las Vegas is almost three thousand miles from here. You and me in a car for three thousand miles? Come on." Then again, perhaps I should find a wedding chapel—a drive-through, at that—as soon as possible so that I didn't destroy a good thing. And Tom and I had a good thing. A very good thing. Tom had been there when my mother died. He'd taken care of me. He'd taken care of business. He'd been there for two more years of my life. And we'd both had ups and downs.

Nick, on the other hand, had been my lunch buddy. Had shared his stories about women. About his lack of feelings about the women he dated.

But *he'd* also been there when my mother died. While I'd been waiting for Stella's plane to land at the Portland Jetport, I'd walked over to the huge expanse of windows, stared at the planes coming in, the planes being loaded up with bags. I stood there sobbing. And I called Nick on my cell phone, but got his voice mail and left a message. And very late that night, after Stella had fallen asleep wearing my mother's favorite huge wool sweater, and

Tom had gone home, Nick had knocked on my apartment door with two pints of ice cream, a bottle of Jack Daniel's and two boxes of Puffs tissues. And we sat on the floor in my living room, on the rug, in front of the fireplace, and he told me about the day *his* mother had died, also a car accident. He was thirteen and thought he wasn't supposed to cry but then couldn't contain himself anymore and sobbed through the funeral. His father and older brother held him tight and let him cry without a single shush, and that was what he remembered most. The not being shushed.

What Stella remembered most about our mother's funeral was what I'd said about not loving Tom.

"Aren't you curious to know what Nebraska is like?" she asked now. "If it's all cornfields? We can break the drive into a week, stay along the way, see some really cool sites. I'm *dying* to see the Rock and Roll Hall of Fame and Museum in Ohio. That's just a couple days into our trip! Ruby, you could actually touch the hem of the leather jacket Bruce Springsteen wore on the cover of *Born To Run*."

I doubted you could actually touch it, but I wouldn't mind seeing that leather jacket. Or driving through a cornfield that never ended.

"Come on, Ruby," she said. "School is out. You said all you're planning to do this summer is take a Spanish class and learn to knit. You can do that in the car! You can bring those Berlitz tapes. I'll plan the entire trip—down to where and when to stop for the night. I'll even make all the reservations. We'll stick to a plan, and you know how you like plans. We'll take a week to drive down, spend a week there, and then Tom can fly down, you'll get married if you're really serious about it, and then we'll all drive back. You'll drop me in New York, and then you two can drive back up to Maine and live boringly ever after. Or we can even fly back, and you know how I hate to fly."

"Why do you want to do this so bad, anyway?" I asked, narrowing my eyes at her. "Why do you want to be stuck in a car with me for three thousand miles? Why do you suddenly want to help me pick out a wedding chapel when you think Tom is wrong for me?"

"The plan isn't to pick out a wedding chapel, Rubes. It's to trap you in the car for a couple of weeks. Someone has to try to save you from making the biggest mistake of your life, Ruby. And Grammy Zelda doesn't drive. I'm all you've got."

At least she was honest.

"So, you're going to drive all the way to Las Vegas to convince me not to get married."

"Just say yes, Ruby. I want to make sure I can reserve a really cool car. A convertible. Red."

"Say yes to *what,* exactly? To listening to you tell me that I don't love my fiancé? I don't think—"

She clutched her map. "Okay, so there might be another reason I want to go to Las Vegas," she said, biting her lip. "And I remembered how you said that if you ever got married, you'd want to elope to Las Vegas, so that's why I thought of you, why I figured I'd ask if you were interested in driving there."

I waited for the reason, which seemed slow in coming. Which was worrisome.

"I…uh…I can—what's that cliché? Kill a bird with a stone?"

"Two birds," I said. "With one stone."

"Well, the first bird is your engagement. Which I do plan to kill."

"And the other bird?" I prompted. It was *that* bird that was making me nervous. Did Stella have a gambling problem? Did she owe loan sharks a pot of money or something? Did she want to be a legal prostitute?

"No other bird. That's it." She dropped down on the bed and burst into tears.

"Stella?" I handed her the box of Puffs from the bathroom.

She took a deep breath and wiped at her tears, then squeezed her eyes shut. "Okay, so I'm pregnant and I think the guy, the father, lives in Las Vegas. I'm ninety-nine percent sure that's what he said. I want to try to find him. Okay? Is your answer yes now?" She stood and walked over to the window and stared out, biting her lip again.

I stared at her. Stared at the profile of her stomach, which was flat as always.

"I'm ten weeks, Ruby. Due in December. The second. Isn't that amazing?"

It was our mother's birthday. But she'd died the day before she could turn fifty-four.

Stella's face crumpled. "It was a one-night stand. I don't even know his name. I think it starts with *J.* Jake or James. Jason, maybe."

"Oh, Stella," I said, now really aware what it meant to be unable to form a thought.

She burst into tears again. She stood there and cried and I wrapped my arms around her.

"We had this amazing chemistry, Ruby," she said, her voice cracking. "But we drank so much and kept drinking and then in the morning he was gone, no note with his name and number, nothing. I met him in a bar and I remember he said something about living in Las Vegas and being here—New York—on business. I'm pretty sure he said he was a lawyer. Or maybe not. I can't remember. I wish I could remember." She started sobbing again. "How can I not remember anything about the father of my own baby? How can I do that to my baby? How can I do that after knowing what it's like not to have a father?"

I squeezed her hand. "It'll be okay, Stell."

"Will you help me try and find him?" she asked, sniffling. "In between checking out wedding chapels—I mean, if that's really what you want?"

I had no idea *how* we'd find him, but I nodded. Las Vegas wasn't Blueberry Hills, Maine, with its population of six thousand. How would we find a guy whose name might be Jake or James or Jason, and who might be a lawyer, and who might not even live in Las Vegas? "We'll leave Monday morning," I told her.

It was Saturday. That would give me enough time to pack, to plan—what I didn't know.

I would make her do most of the driving, if that was okay for pregnant women, and I assumed it was. It would do her good to focus on the road. And I could stare out the window at the passing scenery, the passing states. And think. And that would do me good.

I wouldn't have opened the presents, I would have waited till I got back from the trip, but Tom's sisters and aunts insisted. Once the party winded down, and it was just family (Stella feigned a migraine and disappeared into my bedroom with my laptop, to research the route), Caroline handed me a box with a bow. And she kept handing me boxes for almost an hour. Tom and I received great stuff, including a talking scale, exquisite wineglasses and matching kitschy lingerie from Stella.

I lay in bed with the ribbons-festooned paper plate on my head that the Truby women also insisted on making me. Once it was on my head, I couldn't seem to take it off.

"You're lucky I don't know where you keep your scissors," Stella had said earlier, making menacing cutting motions with her fingers.

I was wearing the kitschy nightie. Tom was wearing the matching boxer shorts. Navy-blue silk with cartoonlike lobsters with thought bubbles that said: *Eat Me!* The lobsters were over certain areas, of course. Tom thought they were hilarious. You had to give him credit for that.

It had taken me a while to tell Tom about Stella, about

the situation, the road trip. I'd waited until he came back from driving Zelda and Harry to the nursing home. Then until we'd cleaned up. Then until we had some leftover barbecue chicken, and then until we went upstairs to bed.

"I think it's a great idea," he said, gently yanking a purple bow taped on by my ear. He lay down beside me, smelling of Ivory soap. "Even if Stella doesn't find the guy, which seems kind of a needle in a haystack, you two could use a good, long road trip. You need to work on your relationship once and for all."

"We might murder each other before we hit New Hampshire."

He smiled. "I have a feeling this Stella is going to be a very different Stella than you've ever known. She's pregnant. And alone."

That had to be scary. I'd tried to talk to her all night, but she kept saying she didn't want to talk about it, then finally faked sleeping so I'd leave her alone.

"And I don't know about eloping to Vegas, Ruby," he said, "but if it's what you want…"

Needless to say, I switched the birds. Stella's real bird with the fake bird about checking out wedding chapels, giving that old dream of mine a chance. I couldn't exactly tell Tom that Stella planned to deprogram me for forty-two hours.

"Though, it would be pretty cool to get married in the Elvis Wedding Chapel," he said. "If there really is one. But no Elvis impersonators officiating, okay? They can serenade us, though."

"Deal," I said, finally able to take off the stupid hat. Tom was always able to make things feel okay.

"Anyway, we have plenty of time to talk about that," he added.

I hadn't realized how often he gave that as his final answer. Tom envisioned a big fancy wedding like every Truby had before him. I knew that because he'd said so a few times. I supposed that was how that list of questions in the *New York Times* article worked; at some point you'd have to go from bringing up an issue to actually deciding how you felt, what you could live with, what was a deal breaker. Eloping to Las Vegas or having a fancy schmancy wedding with a ten-tier cake and a band were both good. But Las Vegas was better. For me, anyway.

A deal breaker—a real deal breaker—was being in love with someone else.

Tom's hands were exploring the lobsters, but it was close to two in the morning, and he was asleep in seconds. I ran my hands through his clean brown hair and listened to him breathe. For a moment, all was well in the world. I was with my Tom. He loved me, and I loved him.

And then, as always, Nick's face, his body, his voice, was all over me. I hadn't spoken to him since the party. And I wouldn't call him or go see him before I left Monday morning. It didn't matter—okay, it *shouldn't* matter—if Nick was serious, if he really meant it, if he really had feelings for me. What mattered was how I felt. And I had no clue.

3
————————————————

STELLA CRAVED CHOCOLATE MALT BALLS, TEN CARTONS OF WHICH she had in the car—a red convertible like she wanted. She kept a bunch of the malt balls in the cup holder between us.

"I am dying for a McDonald's hamburger," she said, a malt ball puffing out her cheek. "Not Burger King or Wendy's. It has to be McDonald's. And I want extra ketchup. A ton of ketchup."

She was in luck because there was a McDonald's every half hour between here, which was still Maine, and Las Vegas. It was only eleven o'clock. We hadn't even been driving an hour, hadn't even hit the New Hampshire border. So far, so good, though. Sort of. We hadn't had a single fight, even though Stella had answered every one of my questions with *I don't know.*

Including: *Where exactly are we looking for Jake or James or Jason?*

Usually, I'd come at her with my *Stella!,* but as long as the place we were looking took a long time to get to, that was all I needed to know.

I hadn't eaten in McDonald's in years, but the idea of a cheeseburger and fries and a Coke sounded so good. Stella ordered two hamburgers, fries, a strawberry milk shake, and apple dippers "for the baby."

"I guess I'll be huge in a month at this rate," she said.

Stella was five foot seven and 117 pounds. This I knew because she'd announced her weight this morning and logged it in her pregnancy journal, which she'd been keeping since she'd gotten the news last week.

She'd known for a week and hadn't told me. I had serious feelings for another guy and didn't tell her. What were we supposed to talk about for three thousand miles?

"Omigod, are you those twin kiddie stars who don't look alike?"

Stella beamed at the teenaged girl behind the counter while I turned red and stared at my flip-flops. "You saw us on *Where Are They Now?*"

"Yes! Omigod, it *is* you!" The girl turned to tell her co-workers that Stella and I used to be famous, but no one cared. Except me, busy cringing. And Stella, preening.

For a few years—almost thirty years ago—Stella and I were in-demand baby models. We were the fraternal twins—one blond with pale-brown eyes, and one dark-brunette with blue eyes—who looked nothing alike except for the same ridiculously big, bow-lipped smile and double dimples. Our faces, those smiles, were on countless baby products, but particularly Goodness Sakes brand.

Though we grew up cute enough (Stella *much* cuter, actually), our modeling days were over by the time we were potty trained. Our family life made it until we started losing our baby teeth. Eric Miller, our father, ran off with a low-level casting agent and exactly ten percent (his fee as our "manager") of our sizable earnings when we were six and just "regular kids." Our mother and grandmother and great-grandmother had an "eh, who needs that lowlife thief!" approach to his abandonment and barely mentioned his name again, unlike everyone else in our Queens, New York, neighborhood way back when.

Which was why we moved to Maine. After reading in a magazine like *Life* or *Time* that "Greater Portland" Maine was among the top ten places in the country to raise children, and that beaches were to Maine what parking meters were to New York City, Mom packed up me and Stella, her mother, and Grammy Zelda, and moved us to Blueberry Hills (after waiting exactly one year for that "lowlife thief" to return). We stuck out like the boroughs people we were with our Queens accents and interest in playing handball against the sides of people's houses. And so much for blending in and putting our past behind us. My mother told everyone who'd stand there and listen about our glory days and our no-good father. But Mainers weren't interested in former child stars and their tabloid families. They cared about when the tide was coming in, if your kid was allergic to peanuts, and whether or not this winter would be as bad as the last. And so within a month, we settled in with our new fleece sweatshirts and shiny forest-green Subaru as though we'd always lived in Maine. Come summer we learned how true it was about the beaches.

A few years ago, Stella had spent months sending VH1 e-mails and letters and pictures about our former glory as two-year-olds and how we'd make excellent candidates for their *Where Are They Now?* show about the formerly famous and almost famous. Finally, she'd heard back from a producer who wanted to include us in a "former child stars" medley episode. I said no way. Stella green-lighted them, anyway, and they filmed me walking into BLA without my knowledge and interviewed several students and faculty members, none of whom had known about my baby modeling days.

We hadn't spoken for two months after that argument. "It's no one's business where we are now!" I'd yelled at Stella, but she'd thought it would lead to at least ten minutes of fame for her (it didn't) or maybe even our father knocking on our door (he didn't).

"He'll see what he missed out on and grovel to come back in our lives," Stella had said.

Intellectually, I knew that Eric Miller hadn't left because our careers ended. I knew it was about him, his lack of *some-thing.* According to my relatives his problem was reality; he couldn't deal with it. The reality of family life, of him having to earn a living instead of relying on his daughters. I stopped thinking about it a long time ago. Stopped thinking about it *often,* anyway. But Stella brought it up a lot. Which I understood. How were you supposed to make peace with it? How could you form it, phrase it, reduce it in your head so that it was okay, so that it didn't mean your father didn't love you? *Oh, my dad? Dunno. I haven't seen or heard from him since I was six, but that's okay. He just wasn't the dad type, you know? And I've moved on!* What were you supposed to move on from?

Stella used to scream this when we were teenagers. *What am I supposed to say?* she'd yell at me, as if it were my fault, as if I knew the answer when friends, neighbors would casually ask where our father was. *Where am I supposed to tell people he is?*

"Omigod!" the girl shrieked for the tenth time. "Will you read my face?"

"On the house," Stella said, winking at her, and the girl announced she was on break and led Stella to a table under a giant poster for a free coffee between 5:00 and 8:00 a.m.

During her three seconds of airtime on *Where Are They Now?,* Stella had claimed to be a professional muse and face reader. Her ability to read faces was particularly important for her role as muse, she'd said, because she could, simply by studying the face and its expressions in a two-minute period, instantly pinpoint what was potentially blocking the artist she was working with.

Substitute wealthy male lover for artist.

I munched a long, skinny French fry and watched her stare at the teenager's fresh-scrubbed face. Stella just looked at her, her own expression neutral, and within ten seconds of being stared at, the "truth started to show" on the girl's face. That's what Stella called it. According to my enterprising twin sister, if you sat across from someone and stared at them without speaking for longer than fifteen seconds, the person would begin to squirm. Would begin to feel as though Stella could see inside her, as though Stella *knew*. And within a minute, what was bothering—or thrilling—the person would appear via expression, be it worry or joy or fear or anger, giving Stella her in.

The girl started biting her lip. Her gaze darted from Stella's stare to the poster to me to the employee who'd taken her place behind the register. Back again. Then tears welled up in the girl's eyes and she wiped them away with a napkin.

"You're clearly upset about something," Stella said in her gentle voice.

For this, a ten-minute "face reading," Stella would normally charge fifty bucks. And the sucker would gladly pay!

The girl sniffled. "My boyfriend dumped me because I won't—" she leaned closer to Stella and whispered "—give him a blow job."

Stella nodded and studied the girl for a moment. "That happened to me once. When I was a junior in high school."

"I'm a junior!" the girl said, brightening.

Stella studied her from several angles. "Yup, it's clear. That guy was *so* not the one. You totally did the right thing by not wasting your first experience with him. Excellent!"

The girl beamed. "How will I know when it's the right guy?"

Now it was Stella's turn to lean in. "There won't be a moment's hesitation. You won't have to think about it. Won't be grossed out by the thought of it. Everything will feel right. That's how you don't end up regretting something, even if it ends up not working out."

The teen stared at Stella. She was clearly hoping Oh Wise One would keep talking forever. But Stella was done. "Omigod, you are so good." She leapt up and ran over to her co-workers behind the counter. "Omigod! Guys! I totally get it now!"

Huh. I had to hand it to Stella. Not bad, sister dear.

"That depleted my energy stores," Stella said, grabbing the fry out of my hand. "And what I told her goes double for you," she added as we headed back to the car. She stopped to take a sip of her milk shake. "The knowing part. The not regretting."

"Did I ask for a face reading? If I did, my expression would say, 'people who offer unsolicited advice are annoying.'"

"Whatev," she said, unlocking the driver's side. Guess she wasn't tired of driving yet. Which was fine with me. She tended to talk more when she wasn't behind the wheel. "I'll bet he saw it," she said.

"Who saw what?"

"Our father. I'll bet he saw the *Where Are They Now?*

show. Or someone told him about it. Actually, he probably makes sure to watch each episode, just in case we were ever featured."

I shrugged. I had no interest in talking about Eric Miller. What was the point? For a long time, our father's abandonment was all Stella and I had in common, so it was what we talked about. Even as six-year-olds, we spent hours discussing every possible scenario, wondering out loud *why*, *how* until our answers began to irk the other and we stopped talking about even that. Stella had created a fairy tale of how our father had fallen madly in love with the beautiful casting agent, who must have despised little girls and wanted to lock us in a dungeon, and our father loved us so much that he left us behind forever to save us.

Right. Sure. The way I saw it, our father just didn't love us enough. Or just didn't care. That infuriated Stella, but wasn't it the truth? To this day, Stella still believed in the wicked stepmother-dungeon story. And I still went for the he-just-didn't-give-a-shit route.

"You know, Ruby, the fact that you won't talk about it means it bothers you," she said, taking a bite of her hamburger. "So you might as well talk about it."

"What's to say?" I asked, squeezing ketchup on my fries. "Eat before your food gets cold, Stella."

"Ugh, I told her I wanted extra pickles! There's, like, one pickle on this hamburger."

"You can have mine," I said, taking the top of the bun off my cheeseburger, where four pickles were mushed into a dollop of ketchup.

"She gave you my pickles," Stella said, picking them off and laying them on her hamburger.

I'd much rather talk pickles than about our father. "Do you crave pickles?" I asked her. "I thought that was just a joke, a cliché about pregnant women."

"Actually, I only crave malt balls and the entire McDonald's hamburger experience. I just happen to love these little pickles."

She turned on the radio, to a classic rock station, and we ate to *Dream On, Wish You Were Here,* and *Freebird.* Stella ate all her fries and most of mine, too. The only thing she said while eating was that she couldn't think of a single band, rock or otherwise, that had come out of Maine. I reminded her that Patrick Dempsey was from Maine, and we agreed that he was enough.

My cell phone rang just as she pulled back on to I-95. Tom. We had a half-minute checking-in, how's-the-driving-going conversation.

When I put my phone away, Stella fiddled with the radio, searching for a song she liked. She slid in a Jack Johnson CD. "So this morning while you were in the shower I asked Tom how was he going to live without you for two weeks and you know what he said?"

I knew what he said because he'd posed the question rhetorically last night in bed, his hands cupping my face, his eyes full of all good things looking into mine. And then he'd answered, and I had no doubt he'd told Stella the same thing.

She took a sip of her milk shake and licked her lips. "He said you were always right here and put his hand over his heart. Not bad."

I smiled. "Told you."

"So why *don't* you love him?" she asked. "And don't say it was two years ago that you said that. I can tell you don't, Ruby. You're *loving* to him. But you don't love him. Not the way you loved Mark Feeler. I just wonder why. If he's such a great guy."

She was bringing up Mark Feeler? I was madly in love with Mark Feeler when I was *thirteen*. Well, when I was thirteen until I was seventeen. He'd lived next door and was a year ahead of us in school (and he'd gone to the public regional schools, not BLA). I followed him around, unknowingly a pest. Mark was in a band, and I, their most ardent groupie, would race home after school to watch them practice in the Feeler garage. When no one else was around, we'd have long make out sessions. He always tried for more, sticking his hand up my shirt or unzipping my jeans. I usually let him. It never went farther than that, and when I was fifteen and sixteen, he had a succession of girlfriends of whom I was incredibly jealous. I tried to adopt their look, but I couldn't. Stella had it, that sense of style, and she might have been interested in Mark, but she'd had the same boyfriend from age fourteen until the summer she graduated from high school. There was no one else for her but that boy, a wild child named Silas, whose joie de vivre had caught up with him.

One day, when I was sixteen, I found Mark crying in the garage behind the drums. He stopped the second he saw me approaching. He told me his girlfriend had dumped him but he didn't care because he liked *me,* then put my hand on his zipper. He'd used every lie and line there was, like *it hurts so bad* (his heart and his case of "blue balls," which I fell for) and *I really think we're meant for each other.* And after asking him if he would attend the BLA junior prom with me and getting an "I would love to be your date," I gave Mark Feeler my virginity, on the dirty shag rug behind the drum set. Stella had lost her virginity to Silas when she was fourteen, but I still didn't tell her. I wanted to be the only one who knew, the only one who felt the way I did, the only one who had that kind of physical and emotional connection to someone.

By dinnertime, when I'd been writing *Ruby Feeler* in hearts on my notebooks and twirling around my room, Mark was getting back together with his girlfriend. And by the end of the week, when I asked him for the tenth time if he'd still attend the prom with me (he'd brushed me off all week), he told me to stop bothering him already, that he was sorry he "literally and theoretically screwed" me and if he'd known I'd moon around after him every minute for the rest of his life, he never would have touched me. He wasn't going to my stupid prom and he had a girlfriend, so he'd appreciate if I "left him the fuck alone."

Stella had heard most of that. She'd been standing outside the garage, sent by my mother to find me and get to the bottom of why I'd been such a mopey mess all week. I hadn't even realized Stella was in the garage until a guitar hit the wall an inch from Mark's head, which had been her aim. She grabbed another guitar, and he grabbed the fire extinguisher and started spraying at us. We ran out, then he hit the button that electronically lowered the door.

I'd fallen to my knees on the driveway, white crud all over me, sobbing, and Stella lifted me up under my arms and practically dragged me into our house, upstairs to our room and put me in the bathtub, fully clothed, where I cried uncontrollably for a half hour. Stella sat there on the floor, her back against the tub, telling me over and over how sorry she was, that Mark Feeler was a loser jerk and would get his some day, that karma always took care of scum buckets.

By the time our mom had come in and asked why I was taking a bath with my clothes on and what was that white stuff all over Stella, Stella and I looked at each other and actually smiled.

Mark Feeler left for college that fall, and his parents sold the house the following summer, so I didn't have to see him much and then I never saw him again.

There won't be a moment's hesitation. You won't have to think about it. Won't be grossed out by the thought of it. Everything will feel right. That's how you don't end up regretting something, even if it ends up not working out.

I supposed Stella was right about that. I didn't regret losing my virginity to Mark Feeler, despite what happened. Before I knew what a jerk he was, I'd been madly in love.

I sipped my Coke and stole one of her malt balls. "There's a big difference between being sixteen and being twenty-nine."

"Being in love feels different depending on your age?" she said. "I don't think so."

"Stella, what I cared about at sixteen and what I care about now are very different."

"I'm not talking about that. I'm talking about the *feeling*. Not the reasons."

"Stell, if two men wanted to marry you tomorrow, who would you pick—a guy who you couldn't stop fantasizing about, or a guy who would make a great father and a dependable, loving husband, a life partner?"

"Neither," she said. "I'd hold out for the combo."

"I mean, in your current state. Pregnant. As in you have more than just yourself to think about."

"I'd still hold out for the combo," she said. "Why do I choose between either? And do you?"

"I'm not settling for Tom. Tom's everything I ever wanted in a husband. He's what I used to dream about, Stella." And that was true. I used to dream about someone who wouldn't leave, who loved me that much.

"You used to dream about your white knight getting off his horse in Dockers and a crooked tie?" She raised an eyebrow. "Right."

"I'm talking about security. Feeling safe. Knowing heart and soul that it's forever. Unlike our father. Unlike stupid Mark Feeler. Unlike any guy I dated before Tom."

"So, you're saying if any of those guys had proposed, you would have said yes?"

I hated when we spoke different languages. I wasn't sure if she was being bitchy or if she really didn't understand. "Stella, I didn't say yes to Tom because he asked. I said yes because I want to spend the rest of my life with him. And not just because he makes me feel safe. I can talk to Tom about anything, open up about how I'm feeling—*and* still feel safe."

She laughed. "Like you have anything to tell him? You don't even jaywalk, Ruby. Please."

I rolled my eyes at her. What was the point of trying to talk Tom with Stella? Nick's face floated into my mind and I blinked him away, focusing instead on the license plate of the car in front of ours. I glanced at Stella and was surprised to see her gnawing at her lower lip. Something she only did when she actually was deep in thought. "Do you think you'll ever love someone the way you loved Silas?" I asked. I tried to picture him as he might be now, twelve years later at twenty-nine, but only the seventeen-year-old boy he'd been, with his slightly too long hair and those gorgeous blue eyes and his ever-present *Question Authority* T-shirts, which he made and sold for ten bucks each, came to mind.

She shot me a dirty look. "You can't use him as an example. No one will ever compare or have a chance to compare. He died, Ruby."

There were the rocky cliffs and the Atlantic Ocean and

a sign that said *Swim At Your Own Risk,* and Silas was a risk taker. Stella hadn't been with him that day. We'd graduated from high school a few weeks before, and Stella and I and our mother had gone to the outlets in Freeport to shop for Stella's big trip; she and Silas were going to backpack through Europe for the *year.* In that relationship, Stella was the checkpoint, which made both me and my mother nervous—Stella? The more cautious? The more responsible? But they were *StellaandSilas,* and Stella had insisted that she would go to culinary school when they returned from their year of seeing the world and become a major chef in New York City, where Silas would study filmmaking at NYU.

She didn't cry, as she often did whenever Silas's name came up. She just put her hand to her belly and closed her eyes for a moment, then sipped at her milk shake.

I stared out the window at the passing trees and cars, already wishing I was back home, a stack of novels beside me on the porch swing. Tom beside me on the porch swing. The first weeks after school ended were always my favorite of the entire summer; it meant two delicious months were ahead of me, a lazy Maine summer of swimming in the ocean and taking a continuing education class in something interesting like Ancient Greek Civilization or Knitting For Beginners. But now two or three weeks of who-knew-what stretched out in front of me.

Stella wanted to stop at the outlets in Kittery, at the border of Maine and New Hampshire. "I only packed yoga pants, a bunch of tank tops, my flip-flops, and my Sevens. I need a few cute light cardigans and a dress and shoes. You don't think I'll pop in the next few weeks, do you?"

"A pregnant teacher at BLA didn't start showing until she was almost five months along," I told her.

"Good, because I'm not ready to shop in Maternity World," she said as we headed for a kiosk with maps of store listings and locations. "It's weird—I want to stay skinny *and* have a big pregnant belly already. I want evidence that the baby is in there. Do you remember Mom's story about the first time she felt us kick?"

She'd been alone in the apartment in Queens. Our father hadn't come home that night (she'd told us this when we were adults) and she was feeling so alone. And then she felt two swift kicks. Simultaneously. She said she never felt alone after that.

I smiled at my sister and gave her a hug. "No matter what, Stella, you always have me. You know that, right?"

"Duh," she said, opening the door to J. Jill.

Our mother had loved these outlets. She liked the road trip down to Kittery, the shopping, the lunch, the more shopping, and the girl talk on the way back. Once Stella had moved to New York City, my mom and I hadn't gone as often, but we headed down twice a year for new winter and summer clothes. I hadn't been back since her death. Hadn't bought any new winter clothes that season, let alone summer clothes. I tended toward classics with the occasional trendy piece thrown in, so my old wardrobe held up okay.

I ended up buying a sundress and let Stella talk me into buying red espadrilles that tied slightly up the ankles. Stella got two dresses, a slinky red sleeveless wrap dress that would likely accommodate her for the next few months, and a sundress like mine. We also bought two fun straw hats that tied under the chin so our hair wouldn't blow around in the convertible.

Back in the car, in the parking lot, Stella whipped off her white tank top, embroidered with Are You Talkin' To Me? across her chest, and put on one of the new tanks she'd bought, pale pink with Hot Mama written across the front in rhinestones. She certainly was accepting of her situation. And didn't have a modest bone in her body. Granted, we always put the top up when we stopped, but still, there were *windows*.

I ripped off the tag for her. "Stella, there is something I need to know. Are you sure that Jake or James or Jason, or whatever his name is, is the father? Not the artist?"

Last I heard, in her "professional muse" capacity, Stella was working as a nude model for an artist with a wealthy wife. According to Stella, he paid well. Six months living expenses in advance, and Stella lived in New York City. I didn't pry and press into Stella's life the way she did into mine, but since the artist was in his fifties and married with children, I had asked her if there was sex involved, and she'd said yes in an angry tone, then changed the subject. In other words: *Don't judge me, you sanctimonious bitch.*

"I'm sure," she said. "I haven't seen Jeffrey in three months."

"You quit?" I asked, wondering how she was supporting herself. Fifty-dollar face readings couldn't add up to rent in New York City.

We'd each received half of what our mother's house had gone for. It had sold immediately, for which I'd been grateful. I'd needed new people in it so that even if the outside was the same white antique cape with the black shutters and red door, the inside was different, the walls painted other colors, the furnishings someone else's. It would then cease to be our mother's house; her spirit was in her choices, her furnishings, her decor, her color schemes.

Still, Stella had received that money two years ago and had done a lot of traveling the year following our mom's death. She'd even gone to India, to an ashram. Though I supposed there wasn't much call for money on an ashram. She'd also gone to several European countries that year to follow U2's concert tour, then settled in Dublin for six months to be "spiritually closer to Bono."

And the "sizable earnings" earmarked for her college education had been spent in the years immediately following high-school graduation. After Silas died, Stella had stayed home, in bed, for a month. My mother and I had sat at her side when she'd let us, brought her food when she'd eat it, and just let her cry and cried with her. I was supposed to be a counselor at a sleepaway camp in the Berkshires that summer with my friend Amy, but I'd canceled. In early August, Stella said she was moving to New York to go to culinary school, just as she and Silas had planned.

And she did enroll at the Peter Kumps cooking school, but she dropped out after a month and used her money to bankroll her fleeting interests. For a year it was a novel that didn't progress past page fifty-four. Head shots every few months for acting jobs that never panned out, except for an occasional "real person" commercial and a stint doing corporate videos about supervisor-employee relations. And then it was airline tickets and hotel suites. Our mother always said that Stella would find her way when it was her time.

"I didn't quit," Stella said as a sign welcomed us to New Hampshire. "I was sort of fired. His wife walked in on us."

I glanced at her. "What happened?"

"She came charging in with a bucket full of cold water and dumped it all over me, screaming 'I knew it!' and that I was a 'piece of shit whore' over and over again. And then she told me to get out of her house, using every expletive imaginable. She threw something at me, too, a little statue, I think. It hit me in the back and left a huge bruise." She shot me a glare. "Don't look at me like that, Ruby. I hate that."

"I'm not judging you, Stell," I said. But I was.

She sent me the usual eye roll. "Anyway, that was the end of that. I missed him for a long time after."

"You were in love?" I asked. I'd figured it was about the money.

She shrugged. "I don't know. I felt something. But I liked the crazy part of it, too. I liked that he paid my way, that I was his muse. There are two paintings of me in a very important gallery right now."

"Didn't it bother you, though? That he was married? A father? I'm just trying to imagine why you—why anyone— would be interested in someone who was cheating on his family. I mean, to me, it just makes that person immediately unworthy. A slime bucket. I judge *him*."

She was quiet for a moment. "I don't know," she said, settling her huge white pearly sunglasses in front of her eyes. "I don't want to talk about it. Let's put our hats on," she added, pulling over onto the shoulder and reaching into the shopping bag.

We put our hats on, which did help with the hair-flying problem. And then *I don't want to talk about it* became her answer to most questions between New Hampshire and the Massachusetts border, where she got another milk shake, chocolate this time, and we used the bathroom. She did not want to talk about "the baby." She did not want to talk about Jake or James or Jason. She did not want to pose what-ifs.

"What does it feel like?" I asked her, anyway. "Being pregnant. Physically I mean. And mentally."

"I don't know."

"Does it hurt? Can you feel something fluttering in your belly?"

"Nope," she said. "According to that book you got me, I'm not going to feel anything for a while."

The morning after she told me she was pregnant, I'd gone to Blueberry Books and bought us both a copy of *What to Expect When You're Expecting*. On the inside front cover, I wrote: *For my sister, Stella Leigh Miller. With love, Ruby.* I wasn't sure she'd bother reading the book, if she was really taking the prenatal vitamins she said her OB had prescribed. She had asked her OB if her McDonald's cravings were okay for the baby, and apparently the doctor okayed three trips per week, but only plain hamburgers, a small fries and better yet, the apple dippers or one of their salads.

"Do you—"

"Ruby, I don't know and I don't want to talk about it right now."

Of course she was scared. I tended to forget that about Stella. My sister had long been the brazen one, the Miller twin who'd throw musical instruments at heartbreakers. But in this she was out of her element; there was no context, no fallback. No owner of the other chromosomal letter, even.

I glanced at Stella's profile, at the bit of eye I could see through the sides of her sunglasses. Stella had the longest eyelashes, even unenhanced with mascara they were still long. Not that she was unenhanced. Stella liked her makeup. Powder, bronzer, a shimmery sheer red lipstick. Eyeliner and mascara. I was so fair-skinned and blond (though a honey-blond, not white) that too much makeup, any *color,* made me look clownish, so I stuck to brown mascara and a little bronzing powder and clear lipgloss.

Stella was older than me by two minutes and twelve seconds, and she looked exactly like our father. But something told me that her child would look exactly like her and not Jake or James or Jason. Even if we did find the owner of the other chromosomal letter, even if he did materialize into a real person with one definite first name, the baby would look just like Stella.

We stopped for gas and for fresh sodas—me a Diet Coke and Stella a ginger ale—and to use the bathrooms and switch places in the car. As I took the driver's seat, Stella lowered the back of the passenger seat so she could recline, her feet up on the dash.

"So did you and Tom ever figure out how many kids you're going to have?" she asked, sipping her soda.

I envisioned quadruplets crawling around the living room. Four babies. Four. Four. Four. I opened the window and gulped in some of the clear warm air. I tried to blink two of the babies away, but the harder I tried, the more their faces became distinct.

"Guess not," Stella said. "Oh, wait, I mean, guess you're still having four."

"I think the person who wants fewer kids wins," I said. "Anyway, we'll compromise, Stella. That's what a relationship, a marriage, has to be based on. Neither person can demand and insist on his or her way."

"Do you ever get your way?" she asked.

"Of course," I said, and that was true. Tom, who liked modern and brand-new and stainless steel appliances, had wanted for us to buy a house of our own, new construction, instead of moving into my mini-Victorian, but my place meant so much to me that he said he'd gladly live there forever if I wanted.

"Right. So you're having four kids," she said. "At least mine will have lots of cousins," she added, patting her belly.

"At least we're in agreement on names," I told her. "On our first date, we both said we always thought we'd name our daughter Scout, after Scout from *To Kill a Mockingbird,* our favorite book, but that we couldn't because Demi Moore did."

"You were naming your kid on your first date?" she asked, eyebrows raised. "God, what took you so long to get engaged?"

"No, I mean we both separately had picked Scout as a name. Long before we met." When Tom and I adopted Marco from the pound, we thought about naming him Scout, but because he was a boy dog, the name would mean something else entirely, conjure up knots and oaths to Be Prepared instead of Harper Lee. "We talk about it in the abstract," I explained. "'When we have kids,' that sort of thing. But no plans to get pregnant right away."

I didn't actually have the "I want to be a mother" feeling yet. I assumed I would one day. During family get-togethers with Tom's sisters' families, I tried to imagine myself in Caroline's and Anne's places—doing four things at once, while their husbands did one: fired up the grill. The women seemed to be in charge of the kids and the food and the house and the guests, and the husbands were in charge of flipping chicken and brushing barbecue sauce and talking to the guests. Caroline and Anne were both older than I was, but not by much. Maybe when I was thirty-five, I would crave family life.

Then again, Stella wouldn't be doing four things at once while the owner of the other chromosomal letter fired up the grill and chatted with Tom at a barbecue. Over her dead body. She always said you made the life you wanted. But what about circumstances? Like her current ones. Where did they fit into that theory?

I was with Tom because I wanted to be, marrying him because I wanted to, wanted the life I would have with him. As opposed to the life I would have with Nick, which would last for all of two weeks.

What if, what if, what if, what if, what if….

Stella crunched on a malt ball. "Well if you do end up marrying Tom despite not really being in love with him, I'm sort of hoping you'll get knocked up soon so the cousins will have each other."

"Stella, I'm getting really sick of telling you that I do love him, okay?"

"So stop saying it. Speak the truth instead."

I had an urge to pull the strings at her neck very tight. "Why don't we just listen to music and not talk. Put Jack Johnson back on."

Jack Johnson's voice soothed from the speakers. He was the perfect choice. It was almost impossible to listen to Jack Johnson and feel stress.

"Tell me three great things about Tom," she said. "Explain to me why I shouldn't have overlooked all those nice guys."

"I could tell you three thousand great things about Tom."

Huh. I could probably only tell her *three* great things about Nick. And I could probably say the same three things about Tom, well, maybe about two of them. They were both gifted teachers, for one. I'd observed both of them in action, and Tom actually had been able to leave many of his students slack jawed over a segment on multicultural poetry. Hands waving in the air to give opinions and ask questions.

"Okay, so gimme one."

Incredible teacher would mean nothing to Stella, who thought education was best gotten outside of a classroom. "I can count on him, really count on him," I told her. I couldn't say the same for Nick. I was his best friend, but he wasn't mine.

"Tom would fight to the death for you?" she asked. "Jump into a pit of fire?"

"Yup, I am absolutely sure he would."

"Silas was like that," she said. "That's a good one. But, you know, Ruby, I also wanted to rip his clothes off every minute. Do you feel that way about Tom?"

"I think he's sexy," I told her. And I did. He was sexy. In a Clark Kent kind of way. Part of Tom's appeal was knowing how hot he was under those sweater-vests. How good he actually was in bed.

"Really?" she asked, peering at me as though I'd said I found Danny DeVito sexy.

I elbowed her and turned up Jack Johnson. As the red convertible passed signs for Boston and Worcester, I realized that Stella had fallen asleep. I turned down the music. The plan was to drive all the way to Syracuse, New York, almost nine hours altogether, and then stop for the night.

I was so relieved she couldn't talk, couldn't ask questions.

We switched places again just outside of Albany. I tried to read *What To Expect,* "Month 2," but Stella was a constant lane-changer and I gave up. I dozed off for a while and woke up alone in the parking lot of a convenience store just as Stella was returning to the car. She'd gotten me a bag of gummy worms, which I appreciated, and she popped malt balls until signs for Syracuse began appearing.

"I'm so ready to stop for the night," she said. It was barely eight-thirty, and just beginning to get dark.

"So where are we staying?" I asked. "Right in Syracuse?"

"Near the university," was her response.

Near the university turned out to be *I didn't make a reservation so let's just find a place near the school, I'm sure there are tons.* And there were. But she said she planned the whole trip. Which meant I'd be planning the *rest* of the trip.

We found a decent-looking motel next door to a packed bar and grill called Chumley's. Stella flirted with the waiter, who couldn't be older than twenty-one. With one "you look so familiar," he got the whole story about the famous Miller babies and how he'd probably seen us on *Where Are They Now?,* but he hadn't. He did get a face reading, which paid for our dinner, and Stella's phone number from when she briefly lived in Boston during her early twenties. Apparently, Stella hadn't paid for a meal—or given out her real number— in years.

★ ★ ★

Our motel was standard issue: small, two twin beds with two end tables and two ugly lamps. Stella dropped onto the bed closest to the bathroom, which made sense, and was snoring in three seconds. I took my *What To Expect,* my cell phone, and the room key and headed out to the pool area a few feet from our door. The pool was dark and deserted and creepy, a dozen or so seen-better-days chaise longues dotted around. A huge black crow was pecking at something on the far side of the pool.

I lay on the chaise, wishing I'd thought to bring a towel. The backs of my thighs immediately stuck to the plastic. It was much hotter here than in Maine, more humid. But the tiny bugs and mosquitoes were exactly the same. I batted a few away with my book and then called Tom on my cell phone.

It was nice to hear his voice. Reassuring. Back home, things were as they should be. Tom was teaching two summer school classes, and they'd started today, plus he was getting a certificate in a graduate classics program at Bowdoin. He was busy.

"Marco misses you," he said. "He's laying at my feet in the living room, staring at the front door."

I smiled to think of Marco and the silly dog faces he made. Marco was an older beagle and had a sad, drooping expression. When Tom had first met Stella, he paid her the fifty bucks to read Marco's face, and after studying Marco from every angle, she reported that he wasn't sad at all, that he was perfectly content, wished for more Scooby Snacks or whatever dogs ate for treats, and just had a sad face. Tom had a soft spot for Stella from then on, despite her shabby treatment of him. He always went overboard to treat Stella like a treasured guest, which annoyed her to no end. Despite already having two sisters, Tom was thrilled about getting another. This morning, he'd peppered her with questions as she ate her ridiculous Quisp cereal (she'd brought her own box), her favorite as a kid.

"So, Stella, what are you up to these days?" he'd asked.

"I'm actually working on a novel," she'd said, in between crunches, then shot me a *Could he be more banal?* glance. "About diner waitresses around the country."

"Really!" Tom had said, pouring a cup of coffee for me. "That's fascinating. What's your thesis?"

Crunch. Crunch, crunch. "At this point, I'm just interviewing. I'll figure it out when I sit down to write." Crunch.

Stella had long been interested in diner waitresses. Not waitresses in metropolitan areas, the ones that bored her with their head shots tucked into their apron pockets. But real live waitresses from the US of A. Waitresses who were waitresses and not models, actors or writers. Waitresses who were more likely single mothers.

It had once been Stella's dream to be a roving diner waitress, work in every state in the country and then write a memoir. She'd actually gotten through a few states. She'd be on vacation somewhere, lie about needing a job, get it, and then work one shift and quit. If she was planning on actually interviewing diner waitresses during this cross-country trip, she'd already missed a few golden opportunities. Unless cute bar-and-grill waiters counted, which I assumed they didn't.

I heard the sound of giggling in the distance and switched my cell phone to my other ear. Tom reminded me to take my one-a-day vitamin, which I always forgot, wished me pleasant dreams, and we hung up. The phone rang a second later, and I assumed it was Tom calling back to remind me of something else, but it was Nick. I bolted upright.

"Hey," he said, and just that word alone sent tiny sparks shooting up my back. "There's something I want to know."

I waited.

"Did you leave because of me?"

"Actually, no," I said. "Stella and I have been planning this trip for a while." A harmless fib, I figured.

"Tell me something, Ruby. Is there a chance?"

I could picture Nick, lying down on his massive brown leather couch in front of the floor-to-ceiling wall of windows in his apartment. No shirt. Army-green cargo pants. Bare feet. His own dog curled up next to him, a skinny mutt named Billy that he'd adopted from the pound. I'd gone with him, and both of us went straight to Billy. That was his name on the little card on his kennel and Nick thought it suited him.

Nick was also teaching summer school, an AP Shake-speare class that would earn the students college credit. The class was going to put on a modern version of *Henry V* at the end.

I closed my eyes. "I don't want to say anything right now, okay?"

I could see him nodding in that way he did. "You'll let me know when you know?"

"Yes," I whispered.

And that was that. I held the phone to my chest for a moment, then lay there, still unable to think clearly, until the mosquitoes chased me away.

As I was heading back to my room, I heard a giggle, then a splash. From the other side of the pool, a guy had dived in. A young woman in a bikini stood by the edge. He swam over and put his hands around her ankles. "C'mon, shimmy out of that suit," he said. "The water is so warm."

I wasn't sure if I should cough or not. She probably wouldn't appreciate discovering she'd stripped in front of a stranger.

But she giggled and dived in, and then her bathing suit, top and bottom, was flung willy-nilly onto the deck. Her top landed on a potted plant. She swam to the edge and he followed her. I thought she was going to climb the metal ladder, but she gripped the sides instead and he pressed against her, both of them breathing very heavily.

I slipped away, back to the room and let myself in. Stella, an inveterate skinny-dipper who often said she loved having sex in the water, despite its difficulty, would have applauded the spontaneity of that little show, but she was still fast asleep, the rhinestones glowing on her Hot Mama tank. I slid the book out from under her head and put it on her end table. The air-conditioning in the room was so cold that I shut it off and opened the windows, listening to the splashes and giggles and Stella snoring. I imagined myself in that pool with Nick. Then tried to morph him into Tom, but it was Nick who won.

4

_____

In the morning, we stopped at a Whole Foods–style deli to pack our lunch and snacks for the trip. As I decided between a red or green apple, Stella announced she had to have a Swiss cheese omelet right then or she would go out of her mind, so we left the deli and headed across the street to a diner. The smiling waitress who came over with a pencil behind her ear and a pad in her apron was both pregnant and not wearing a ring on any of her fingers. As she poured our coffee, Stella asked if she could interview her for a book she was writing.

"I'm on break in five, so I could come sit with you if you want," the woman said. "I'm craving an omelet myself. Western. No, Greek. With a side of chocolate pudding."

Stella looked like she might throw up. She'd always hated

chocolate pudding, mostly because of an episode in elementary school with a rival who'd dumped an entire saltshaker into Stella's little chocolate pudding container.

The waitress, whose name tag announced her name as Jen R., to differentiate her from fellow waitress Jen B., who also hated being called Jennifer or Jenny, served our breakfasts and her own, the Greek omelet, with the side of chocolate pudding right on the plate, next to the home fries.

"So let's start with the basics," Stella said, forking a piece of cheesy omelet into her mouth. "Why don't you just tell me a little about your life, getting as personal or as not as you feel comfortable."

Jen gobbled up half her omelet with one finger up in the air at Stella before she said a word. "I was starving. Been on shift since six, when we opened. Okay, so let's see. My name is Jen Reilly and I'm pregnant with my third child. I have a boy and a girl, seven-year-old John Junior and five-year-old Samantha." She patted her belly. "This here will be either Michael or Moriah. Isn't Moriah pretty? And I love the name *Michael*. You never hear of a baby being named Michael anymore. But how many Conners and Ethans does the world need?"

There were at least five Michaels in every class I ever took growing up. Every now and then a Tom. Lots of Nicks. Stella and I were always the only Ruby and Stella, but both names had gotten popular with the infant crowd.

Stella seemed disappointed that Jen was married and not

a single-mother-to-be from whom she might glean some wisdom or advice. "I'm pregnant, too," Stella whispered. "You're the second person I've told aside from my sister," she added.

"You two are sisters?" Jen said, glancing between us. "You look nothing alike! Hey, so what are you planning to name the baby," she asked Stella. "Do you know if it's a boy or a girl? I guess not yet. You're not even showing."

Names. I'd been so focused on the identity of the father that I almost forgot about the identity of the baby. I hadn't even asked Stella what names she was considering.

Stella slathered half a toasted bagel with butter. "I did have one ultrasound. The doctor said he couldn't tell yet. But if it's a girl, I'm going to name her after our mother," she added, eyeing me. "And if it's a boy, Silas, after someone I once knew."

"There are three Silases in John Junior's kindergarten class!" Jen said. "What's your mom's name?"

"Clarissa," I answered, sending a smile to Stella. I loved that name. The world definitely needed more Clarissas.

Stella had offered Jen a free face reading, but Jen said she didn't go for that type of thing, that it was against her religion. As a congratulations, she packed the two of us a lunch on the house, adding a baggie full of pickle spears for Stella.

"Are you really going to write a book?" I asked her as we headed to the car.

She shrugged and bit into a pickle. "Maybe. The research is what's important, though. Asking the questions, getting answers."

"Answers about what? How other people live their lives? That won't help you, Stella. You're you."

"So if I'm me, why are you telling me I should think like you?" She added the Angelina head tilt.

I mimicked strangling her and got behind the wheel.

She needed to interview herself, ask herself some questions. Like I was trying to do with the *New York Times* list of questions. Someone else's marriage, how another couple interacted, the dynamic between them, wouldn't help me figure out how to have a happy marriage of my own.

It was my turn to drive. Today's stop: Cleveland, Ohio, almost six hours away. Because the Rock and Roll Hall of Fame and Museum closed at 5:30 on Tuesdays (Stella had really and truly called yesterday), we decided to drive straight there, no stops. One thing we could both agree on was that we both wanted to see the leather jacket Springsteen wore on the cover of *Born To Run* and the sexy Levi's, too. Stella wanted to see anything that Bono, her personal God, might have worn or touched.

When we reached the museum, we got as far as the kiosks to listen to the "500 Songs That Shaped Rock and Roll" when Stella put her hand over her mouth. I had Louis Armstrong in my ears when Stella said she was going to be sick, so we raced to the bathroom. We didn't know if it was morning sickness or just Stella being anywhere in the vicinity of chocolate pudding, albeit six hours earlier. She was positively green, so we left the museum, figuring we'd hit it on the way back.

Stella swore she really did make reservations at a lovely bed-and-breakfast near the museum, so I followed her Google Map directions to a house about ten minutes away.

"Are you sure this is it?" I asked. "This doesn't look like an inn. It barely looks big enough to be a house." It was a tiny white saltbox. There was one car in the driveway and one in front of the house. I pulled behind a gray Honda Accord on the street.

"Stella, I don't think—" And then I noticed the name on the mailbox. Miller-Geller.

"Don't be mad, Ruby," she said, looking like she might throw up again. Now I wasn't so sure if she was faking for sympathy.

I narrowed my eyes at her. "Who lives here?"

"Do you remember Aunt Sally by any chance? Our dad's sister?"

I glared at her. "How could I remember someone I've never met? Stella, what are we doing here?"

"I just thought that since we're here, I mean, we could just stop and meet her. Find out something, anything. I don't know."

"About our father?" I asked. "What would she know? She was estranged from him before we were even born."

"But she knew him once. They grew up together. I'm just looking for some light. Insight. Something."

"Fine, you knock on the door. I'm going to find a hotel and take a nap. Bye." I opened the car door, my heart pounding. How dared she?

She grabbed my arm, then rummaged through her bag and pulled out a folded up sheet of paper. "Clarissa, you are the love of my life," she read. "I want to spend every day of the next eighty years by your side. I want to raise a family with you, see your light, your beauty and grace in our children's faces…"

It was the Denny's children's menu that our father had used the back of to write his wedding vows. She must have taken it from my mother's hope chest, which I kept in my bedroom.

"So?" I said. "He didn't mean a word of it. What's your point, Stella?"

"He meant it when he wrote it, Ruby. I believe that. I need to believe that. Something changed, but when he wrote these words, he meant it. I guess I want to know who that person was. Before he changed."

"We're twenty-nine, Stella. He left when we were six. That means twenty-plus years of Eric Miller postchange. What's there to know?"

"God, Ruby, what are you so afraid of? It's *information,*" she said, waving the menu. "It's our past. Our history. I want to know."

"It's a shitty past. But fine, go chase your fairy tale. I'm finding a hotel with a Jacuzzi tub." I started to get out of the car.

"Ruby, I'm pregnant and looking for the father of my baby," she said in such a low voice I could barely hear her. "If I can't find him, I want to be able to tell Silas or Clarissa that I tried to find him, that it wasn't his fault or my fault, that we didn't mean for him or her to end up without a father." Tears pooled in her eyes. "I don't know what the hell I'm even saying." She covered her eyes with her hands.

"I understand what you mean," I said. "I really do, Stell. But I don't know what our aunt is going to tell us that we don't already know."

"Can we just find out? Please? I can't do this by myself, Rubes."

I squeezed her hand. "Okay."

We got out of the car and stared at the tiny house. There were two well-tended pink rosebushes on either side, which was a good sign. You couldn't cultivate a garden if you weren't a nice person, could you?

"Maybe I should change," Stella said, reaching back into the car for her suitcase. She was wearing her jeans instead of the ubiquitous yoga pants, and a tiny white tank top (her uniform). She added the pink cotton ballet-wrap sweater she'd bought at the Kittery outlets and changed from her suede Pumas into pink platform flip-flops.

"Do I look okay?" I asked her, unsure what you wore to meet an estranged relative. An aunt.

"You always look okay," Stella said. "And you're not even wearing teacher clothes."

I smiled. My teacher clothes were just nice pants, like from Ann Taylor or Banana Republic, and a blouse or shirt. I tended to get creative with shoes because I could. Today I looked like Stella. Jeans, a white T-shirt and a pale-lavender cotton cardigan tied around my waist. The shoes were also platform flip-flops, white with little pink hearts dotting the fabric. Tom bought them for me when we first started dating.

We stood there, staring at the house, neither of us moving an inch.

"I'm actually scared," I whispered. "My heart is racing."

"I think we should just go on up and knock on the—"

"Are you lost or something?"

We turned around to find a good-looking guy, early twenties tops, dripping with sweat. He wore a white T-shirt and blue running shorts. He managed to be both ruggedly handsome and pretty-boy at the same time.

"Um, we're looking for the Miller-Geller residence?" Stella said in the form of a question.

He pointed at the little house. "You found it. Who you looking for? I'm a Miller-Geller."

We stared at him. "We're Millers," I said. "Our father was, I mean, *is,* we think *is,* I mean we really don't know if he's alive or dead, actually. How ridiculous is that?" I clamped my mouth shut.

He stared back. "So you're my mother's brother's daughters? The kiddie models? The twins that don't look anything alike?"

At least he knew who we were. "That's us." I pointed at Stella. "That's Stella. And I'm Ruby."

He glanced between us both. "Glad you said so, because I wouldn't have been able to tell you apart."

Stella and I eyed each other.

"Kidding," he said, grinning. "Um, is my mother expecting you? She didn't say you were coming."

"We're passing through," Stella said. "We were at the Rock and Roll Hall of Fame, and since you all live so close, we thought we'd just be brave and knock."

He laughed. "You'll need bravery. My mother has the personality of a crab. At low tide."

"Great," I muttered into Stella's ear.

"I don't know why you bothered to come all this way," Sally Miller-Geller said, setting a plate of scones on the coffee table. "Again, I'm really sorry about the air-conditioning. It was working yesterday. Refill your iced tea?"

Anything for a moment's reprieve from this woman. Her son was right. She was a total crab. I kept waiting to feel something, a familial connection, any sense of family whatsoever. But Sally Miller-Geller might well have been a stranger. Though, I supposed she was.

It might have been easier to feel something if she looked like Eric Miller, but I couldn't tell if she did or not. The few pictures we had of him—the ones my mother specifically saved for our "memory album"—showed a tall, rangy man with dark-brown hair in a sort of new-wave eighties cut, in either a fancy suit or jeans and a white button-down shirt. He had a narrow face, neither of which Stella and I had; we'd both inherited our mother's heart-shaped face. Sally did have the narrow face, too. And frizzy dark hair, all one length to just below her chin, in the shape of a pyramid. She wore tortoiseshell glasses, which she kept adjusting. A nervous habit, I supposed. I wasn't sure of her eye color. Hazel, maybe. Greenish-brownish. Nothing about her features reminded me of my father, what I remembered him looking like.

She returned with the pitcher and topped off our glasses, which we'd hardly touched. Then she disappeared again and returned a moment later. "I don't really see what I can tell you about your father. I haven't seen or heard from him since before you were born."

She said that as though it was normal, as though that was the way families were. And since our paternal grandparents had died before we were born, that would make Eric and Sally all either had left of their nuclear family. How could they just never speak to each other again as though they *weren't* family? I tried to imagine never speaking to Stella again. Though there were times I was thrilled we were on the outs, we both always knew that we'd get together come our birthdays and Thanksgiving and for the anniversary of our mother's death.

"You don't mind staying in one room, do you?" Rory asked, coming in with our suitcases. He'd clearly showered; he now wore a white T-shirt and jeans. "As you can see, it's a pretty small house. You guys can have my room, and I'll sleep down here on the couch."

What? Since when were we staying the night? We couldn't possibly.

Stella opened her mouth to say something, but Sally, looking at her son with a murderous gleam, rushed to say, "Oh, I'm sure Ruby and Stella have reservations at some lovely hotel. Your room is hardly clean for company, anyway, Rory."

"Mom," Rory said in a singsong. "It's fine."

Stella's hand flew to her mouth. "Where's the bath-room?" she asked on a croak, then raced when Rory pointed down the hall.

"Must have been something she ate," I said. I was hardly going to announce Stella's pregnancy and any-time-of-the-day morning sickness to Auntie.

As sounds of Stella's morning sickness or nerves or bad eggs came from down the hall, Sally said, voice clipped, "If she's sick and you want to stay the night, you're welcome to Rory's room. I was just planning on a simple dinner, so…"

"I'll cook," Rory said, smiling so expectantly at me that I didn't have the heart to tell him I couldn't wait to get out of his tiny house.

"Great," I said. "I don't know if Stella will be able to eat, but I guess that's what doggie bags are for."

And that was how—upon Sally's departure to "freshen up" Rory's room—we got on the subject of Marco, who I already missed, and how Rory always wanted to adopt a

German shepherd from the pound. He thought German shepherds were dogs in their truest form.

Stella emerged from the bathroom looking radiant. Had she been faking? To wrangle an invitation to stay? Even though Sally had made it clear that she wasn't going to tell us anything? "So what's your specialty?" Stella asked Rory, and off we went to the kitchen, which was twice the size of the living room.

I'd always envied Stella's ability to do that, to feel at home with anyone, anywhere. As a child, from my earliest memories, Stella would just run in, jump in. To our preschool, to friends, to teachers. As a child, Stella would go from never having laid eyes on someone to whispering secrets in their ears or painting a cat on the sides of their faces. And there I'd be, standing awkwardly next to the teacher, afraid to move, afraid to speak. How were we so different? How could our personalities be so different?

When it came to puberty and boys, Stella just assumed the boys liked her, wanted her to be their girlfriend. And they did. Where did that self-confidence, that self-esteem come from at that age? And at twelve, no less, when developing identity with mixed messages from society, from the media, from your own father's abandonment, was supposed to do a number on you. And if she had confidence naturally, why didn't I? We'd been dealt the same parents, the same home, the same set of circumstances. Our mother loved us both equally, favoring neither. And our father was an equal-opportunity ignorer when he wasn't chastising us both at five and six for throwing jobs. Either Stella didn't pop her dimples enough or I wasn't lifting my chin enough or we were both "not wanting it enough." Back then, we actually *did* want it. We both loved the attention, especially from our father, but really from everyone. At the studios, we'd hear how absolutely adorable we were, how poised, a hundred times. I couldn't recall if our father treated us better in the studios than he did at home, but I assumed he was a lot nicer to us when people were looking.

"I make a mean spaghetti and marinara sauce," Rory said. "I know that sounds simple and boring, but wait until you taste my sauce. I should have my own show on the Food Network." He glanced at us, standing there staring at him. "Sit, sit," he said, gesturing at the round table and chairs beside the window. "Or you can help if you want. I love having assistants in the kitchen, snapping at people to get me the garam masala."

"Are you putting garam masala in the sauce?" Stella asked, eyebrow raised.

Rory laughed. "Only if I wanted to make you throw up again, which I don't. Sometime I'll make you my Indian specialty. Chicken tikka masala."

Stella started telling him about her month at the Peter Kumps cooking school. Rory gave us his history in short form: he had just graduated from college, a business major, but if he had it his way, he would have gone to culinary school in Paris. He counted the Pixar film *Ratatouille* among his favorites, right up there with *On the Waterfront*.

"Not that I'm a rat," he said, smiling. "But I do love to cook."

"So whose way was it?" Stella asked.

Rory peered into the big pot on the stove. Not boiling yet. "My dad. He worked for the same company for thirty-five years. You know the drill. The idea of his son going to cooking school almost gave him a heart attack. So I majored in business and minored in restaurant management. I'll get to culinary school one day. Anyway, I'll know how to open my own restaurant and run it, so that'll be cool."

The water began boiling. Rory put me on breaking-the-spaghetti duty. It snapped with a satisfying crackle.

"You did that like a true chef," he said to me. "What do you do for a living?"

"I'm a teacher. At a private school."

"She teaches at the same school she graduated from," Stella said, slathering two sides of Italian bread with butter. "How's that for stable?"

Rory was peeling a clove of garlic. "Stable's good," he said, winking at me. "And I assume from the ring on your finger that you're engaged?"

I smiled. "To a fellow teacher."

"If she marries him, her name will be Ruby Truby," Stella informed.

"Ruby Truby. I like it," he said. "It's a good rhyme." He set aside the garlic and started chopping tomatoes. "I couldn't help but catch the *if,* though."

"Don't mind her," I said. "She has a problem with nice,

stable people with nine-to-five jobs and retirement plans. Nine to three, I should say. Tom is a great guy."

"He wears tightie whities," Stella whispered to Rory. "I peeked in his side of the dresser. And all his clothes are neatly folded like he works in the Gap. And he has twenty pairs of khaki pants and a hundred sweater-vests."

"He's a Milton scholar!" I said in defense.

Rory laughed. "So what about you, Stella? What do you do from nine to five?"

"From nine to about noon I'm usually still sleeping," she said. "The rest of the time I'm a professional muse and face reader," she added as though she'd said "bank teller" or "lawyer."

"That sounds cool," Rory said. "Can you read—"

A discreet cough announced Sally standing in the doorway. She looked mighty uncomfortable. She clasped her hands in front of her, then behind her, then straightened the trivet, twice, on the stove. "Well, I do have some additional housework to attend to—your visit was unexpected—so…"

So she left, practically running to get away. Rory and his mother were case number two of how different close family members could be.

"Dinner in twenty, Mom," he called after her with a devilish smile at us.

Rory was true to his word. Time wise and his specialty. Delicious. Too bad I couldn't bring some home to Tom. He especially loved good garlic bread, even the kind you bought frozen from the supermarket. Every time he tried to make it fresh, the smoke detectors went off.

We sat in the small dining room, each of us with a glass of red wine in front of our plates, which were heaped with spaghetti and garlic bread. I glanced around the room, trying to get a better sense of Sally, a sense of her personality. I caught Stella doing the same. But there was nothing to glean from the off-white walls or furnishings, which were neither traditional nor modern, neither country nor not. There was some basic wood furniture, a matching sofa and love seat in a natural color. A framed needlepoint of a sailboat hung over the sofa, but I doubted Sally wanted me to ask if she created it or not.

What a difference from my mother's house! The home we grew up in in Maine was so warm and welcoming, so cozy and comfy. There, walls were soft yellows and the palest of blues, the couches and chairs plush with vibrant pillows, the artwork mostly homemade by the three of us over the years. And photographs, big and small, on the walls, the tables, every surface. As I looked around Sally's house, I realized there weren't any photographs, except two graduation shots of Rory behind glass in a hutch.

"So do you have any old photo albums?" Stella asked Sally. "I'd love to see our dad when he was a kid. Our mom said he took all his stuff with him when he left."

"I wouldn't even know where to look," Sally said, twirling pasta that never seemed to make it to her mouth.

We weren't going to crack her. Stella seemed to accept

it, and we got through dinner—all ten minutes of it— without another personal question. Her gaze had drifted to my ring a few times, but she never commented on it or said congratulations or asked when the wedding was.

"Well, you girls must be exhausted from all your traveling," Sally said. "There are fresh linens in Rory's room. It's a double bed, but I guess as twins you're used to sharing."

"I definitely am exhausted," Stella said.

"You'll clean up, won't you, Rory?" Sally said. "I have my book club." At Rory's *of course,* Sally stood, blotted her lips for the twentieth time, and said, "It was nice to meet you girls. You take care." And then she and her purse and hardcover of one of the Harry Potters were gone.

"I guess we made her uncomfortable," I said to Rory. "Was it a mistake that we came?"

Rory shook his head. "She needed it. People who are stuck need to get shaken. And you guys shook her."

I smiled at him, appreciative of how kind he was and how insightful. "Besides, if we hadn't come, if Stella hadn't insisted on knocking on the door, we wouldn't have met you."

He held up his wineglass, and we both clinked.

"So, Rory, about this dad of yours," Stella said as she carried plates to the kitchen. "Where is he? Lodge meeting?"

"He left a few months ago," Rory said. "For a waitress older than my mom at the diner he always went to for practically every meal."

"Oh," Stella and I said in unison. "Well no wonder she's so crabby."

"She was always crabby," Rory said as we all loaded the dishwasher and cleaned the counters and wrapped up the leftovers. "She was crabby on her wedding day—I saw the video. So you guys want to rent a movie?" he asked. "Play Scrabble? You'd probably beat the hell out of me, though. I suck at Scrabble. Do you believe that a girlfriend once dumped me because I was so bad?"

I laughed. "You couldn't be worse than Stella."

"Hey!" she said, waving half a loaf of garlic bread at me.

And so we spent the next two hours playing Scrabble, then charades, but Stella fell asleep on the couch right in the middle of my miming second word, one syllable. Rory scooped her up and carried her up the stairs and put her down on the bed.

"I'll wake you for breakfast," he said on his way out. "Just leave your suitcases by the door and I'll put them in the trunk for you."

"Thanks," I said. "And thanks for making us feel so welcome."

He nodded. "'Night, cuz."

As he shut the door, I smiled. It was nice to have a cousin. Not so nice was having to share a bed with the snoring bed hog. She'd moved from one side of the bed to right in the middle, an arm extended one way, her face turned the other way.

I changed into pajamas, just a T-shirt and my old pink

sweats that reminded me of home (because of the UMaine on the butt), and slid in next to Stella, placing her arm at her side. I took my phone from my bag to check for messages. There was just one, a text message from Tom.

Thinking about you. I texted back a *Me Too.*

And then I lay there thinking about how it was that people could just up and leave, though if Aunt Sally was generally such a porcupine and not so kind to long-lost nieces who wanted absolutely nothing from her but a bit of warmth and a little history, I could possibly understand why she might be difficult to live with. My mother wasn't difficult, though. She was so easygoing, so funny and charming. And such a good cook! So what was my father's excuse?

I tried to imagine Tom, twenty-five years from now, telling me he was leaving me, a suitcase in his hand and a photo of our four kids in the other. I couldn't imagine it, though. Nick, on the other hand, I didn't see sticking around past the next conquest. But then again, who knew how love worked or what moved people? People were shocked by betrayal all the time. Tom could leave and Nick could stick by me for the next fifty years. I tried to envision Nick as an eighty-year-old, but I couldn't.

My cell phone beeped. Another text message. Tom again.

Thinking about meeting you in Las Vegas. Even drive-through chapel would be okay if I get you in the end…

Whoa.

I didn't know what to text back, so I closed my eyes. The

next thing I knew, a sliver of sunlight was peeking through the blue curtains on the window and Stella's arm was across my neck, and Rory was knocking on the door and saying, "Good morning, sleepyheads. Breakfast in twenty."

My mother always liked me and Stella to come to the breakfast table in our pajamas, fresh-rolled out of bed. She thought the preshowered, pre-get-ready-for-the-outside-world person offered them as they really were. But the idea of going downstairs in our jammies with bed head and bare feet didn't seem quite appropriate here.

When Stella and I came downstairs, showered and dressed and even wearing shoes and carrying our tote bags, Sally was coiffed and lipsticked and sipping coffee from a china cup, one pinky up in the air. She stiffened at the sight of us. Which was really too bad. We *were* relatives. Her brother's daughters, who she'd never met, never seen, outside of images of us as infants and toddlers on baby products.

"Good morning," she said in her clipped voice. She really did remind me of one of those guests desperately in need of Dr. Phil's sixty-minute wisdom. She seemed to have a broken spirit, the kind that had been barely held together all her life, but then smashed with one betrayal. I hoped she had a good friend.

"Ooh, muffins," Stella said, eyeing the basket on the table. "Are those chocolate chips or berries of some kind?"

"Mixed berry," Sally said. "I picked them up at the bakery

in town. They're quite good. Rory ran off to the supermarket. We're out of eggs and pancake mix, and he wanted to make something filling to see you off. You *are* leaving this morning, right?"

I felt like taking her hand, looking deeply into her eyes, and promising her that, yes, we were leaving in a half hour tops and that she'd never have to see us or talk to us again. I took a muffin instead and nodded.

"So, Sally," Stella said, "before we hit the road, Ruby and I thought you might be able to tell us a little something about our father, anything really. Why he might have left, just walked out."

Sally's brow furrowed. "As I've said, I really—"

"We lost our mother two years ago," Stella interrupted. "So we can't ask her."

The expression didn't budge. Sally did purse her lips somewhat, then said, "Well, I really don't think you want my opinion. But since you've asked numerous times, I'll tell you. Your father was a selfish lout and I'm sure he still is. Eric never cared about anyone but himself. Last night, when I got home, Rory went on and on about how your father is probably like some kind of superhero to you, and you want to hear that he left for your own good or whatever, but the truth is the truth. Another muffin?" she added, pushing the basket closer to us.

"The Amazing Invisible Man," Stella said, shaking her head at the proffered muffin. "Some superhero."

I took a muffin, my appetite gone, though. "If you

don't mind my asking, Sally, what happened between you and our father?" It was odd to call her just Sally. Somehow it seemed disrespectful. But we could hardly call her *Aunt* Sally.

She sighed and clasped her hands on the table in front of her. "Well, of course we always had a strained relationship, even as children. But when our parents died—in a car accident—Eric tried to hide thousands of dollars of their money from me. He also hid some of their assets. He did things like that his entire life."

Our parents. She was talking about our grandparents. But again, there was no connection; they'd died before we were born, and I didn't remember my father ever talking about them. There were no pictures of them around the house. Eric Miller certainly wasn't much of a family man.

Our silence must have unnerved her, because Sally went on. "It was no surprise when I heard through a cousin that Eric ran off with your bank account after peddling you two as child models. He lived off you, then when no one was interested in you anymore, he stole your money and took off. What a piece of garbage. He never gave a rat's ass about you two." She shook her head, then emptied a packet of Equal in her coffee.

A little harsh there, Auntie. I was all for reality, but there was something to say for Rory's superhero theory. Who wanted to hear, albeit all the proof, that their father didn't care about them?

Neither Stella nor I said anything. I sipped at my orange

juice to have something to do with my hands. Stella seemed close to tears.

"Did you know he cheated on your mother while she was pregnant with you?" Sally asked as though she had to prove her point. "He was constantly cheating. He used the 'I can make you a star' routine, and so many idiots fell for it. Can you imagine being nine months pregnant with twins and knowing your husband is out sleeping with some woman he met in a bar?"

Suddenly Sally was full of information?

"He stuck around for six more years," Stella pointed out, her cheeks red. "So he must have cared about us. And loved our mother."

Sally shook her head again. "He cared about the gravy train. Period. Why your mother put up with—"

"Don't you say one word about my mother!" Stella yelled as she shot up. She grabbed her tote bag and ran out of the room, and then I heard the front door slam.

Sally looked at me for a moment. "I didn't mean to upset her. I told you you shouldn't have bothered coming all this way for information. I could have told you all this on the phone, Stella."

"I'm Ruby," I said, grabbing my own bag and running after my sister.

Stella was in the car, on the passenger side, half boiling mad, half about to cry. "Let's get the hell out of here."

"But we didn't say goodbye to Rory."

"We'll call him," she said. "I have to get away from this house or I might murder her. I swear to God I might kill her."

I checked the trunk to make sure our suitcases were indeed in there. They were.

"Do you want the top down or up?" I asked.

"Up," she said, so I left it as it was. The morning sky was gray, just a hint of sun peeking out. We had no idea what the forecast was, but it looked like rain was coming.

When we were back on the highway, Stella took a mutilated malt ball out of her mouth and let out a very deep breath. "I can't believe her. Do you believe her? What a *bitch!* Like we needed to know he cheated on Mom when she was carrying us? Like I fucking needed to know that?"

"I told you she was a crab," a male voice said from behind us.

I almost crashed into the SUV speeding past us in the fast lane.

Popping up from the backseat was cousin Rory. "I have almost two hundred in cash and more in the bank. I'll pay for gas if you let me come with you." He held up a brown paper bag. "I also have a carton of eggs and Bisquick if you get hungry. And four gorgeous Granny Smiths. Organic, of course."

When Stella finally caught her breath, she said, "You don't even know where we're going."

"Do I care?" he asked. "Just get me out of Cleveland. Or *I* might murder her. It's weird—I had every intention of taking the groceries inside, whipping up breakfast, and then saying goodbye with a 'keep in touch,' but then I just jumped in the backseat of your car and lay down and waited for you to come out and drive away. And here I am. Man, I wish I'd thought to take my iPod for the walk to the store. It's the only thing I'll miss."

Stella smiled at him. "Can I have one of those apples?"

5

AT AN INTERNET CAFÉ JUST OUTSIDE OF SOUTH BEND, INDIANA, we put Rory Miller-Geller in charge of making our next three reservations. Tonight, in South Bend, tomorrow in Chicago (but on the cheap) and the next night in Lincoln, Nebraska. He dutifully headed to the computer stations at the back with his soup bowl of coffee and an overstuffed panini. Not only had he treated for the drinks and food, but he'd filled up the car as promised.

Rory was so friendly and chatty that in minutes he had advice from those sitting around him on where to stay and where not to stay. He'd been told not to miss the Touchdown Jesus mosaic on the Notre Dame football stadium, and to check out the "future birthplace of Captain James T. Kirk" just south of Cedar Rapids, Iowa.

Stella and I sat in overstuffed purple chairs, our lattes (decaf for Stella) and treats and *What To Expect*s on the battered coffee table in front of us. Hundreds of names were written in pen or pencil or carved in with keys into the wood. A tradition, apparently. Stella borrowed the red marker from the teenager who'd just written her and her boyfriend's initials in a heart, and wrote *SM and S or C was here*. I borrowed it next and wrote *Ruby* in tiny letters down the leg. It reminded me of sleepaway camp as a kid and writing our names in toothpaste on the bunk walls.

Rory rejoined us, sitting down on the tattered sofa across from us. "I made reservations at an inn around the corner tonight," he said, signing his own name on the table. "Then we're staying at my friend Popper's apartment in Chicago and then I booked rooms at some little guesthouse in Lincoln, right in the center of everything."

"Popper?" I asked, raising an eyebrow. "Can we trust someone named Popper?"

"Pete Popperscowski. My college roommate. Great guy. I just graduated from the University of Chicago last month. I wasn't going to come back to Cleveland, but then my mom just seemed so…alone, but six weeks with her was way enough."

"What's your dad like?" Stella asked, nibbling at her brownie.

"Henpecked. I'm sure the new girlfriend will drive him crazy, too. She'll probably kick him out and he'll go home."

I raised an eyebrow. "Your mother would take him back?"

He shrugged. "I think she'll allow him the late-life crisis. And I do think he'll be back. It clearly wasn't a one-night stand or some meaningless affair, but it's not love. Real love, I mean."

"Was it real love between your parents?" I asked. How could it be if one of them left? Wasn't the entire point of real love the staying together? The couplehood? The thick and thin, the richer and poorer, the sickness and in health? Or did that allow for screwing up, thinking that over, and then coming back, *accepting* back?

"They usually ate meals in silence," Rory said, "except for my dad asking my mom for more mashed potatoes or whatever. They watched the same TV shows, like *CSI* and *Law and Order.* They went to Home Depot or a craft show on the weekends. But they did all that for twenty-three years. So what's not real love about it?"

Stella and I both nodded; he wasn't wrong, exactly.

"Lemme ask you something, Rory," Stella said, putting down her soup bowl of coffee on the table in front of us. "Do you think you can feel real love on a one-night stand? I mean, if not talking and watching TV for twenty-five years is real love, do you think you can have an amazing connection with a woman you pick up in a bar, if you talk nonstop about everything and everything all night long and feel the most intense attraction you've ever felt?"

He glanced from me to Stella. "Why is it a one-night stand if the couple had an amazing connection and the wild attraction? Doesn't the amazing connection negate the one-night stand? There's gotta be a second date after an amazing connection."

Stella stuck her fork into her brownie a few times. "Well, let's say that you met a woman in a bar, drank a little too much, had this amazing connection—I mean, you both said you even felt the presence of God in the room, but because you drank so much—"

"The presence of God?" he repeated. "That must have been some fuck."

I burst out laughing, but Stella apparently didn't think it was funny at all. She shot up from the table and ran to the back of the café where the restroom was, yanked at the door handle, but it was clearly occupied, so Stella was stuck standing there, her arms crossed over her chest.

"Oops," Rory said to me, grimacing. "Are you guys religious? I didn't mean to offend—"

I put my hand on his arm. "No worries. Guy trouble, that's all."

"Ah. That I know something about. Girl trouble, I mean."

I smiled. "Let me go talk to her."

By the time I said excuse me to four people whose legs or chairs were blocking the aisle along the path to where Stella was standing, the bathroom became free and she disappeared inside. I waited for a moment, then knocked. "Can I come in?"

She pulled open the door. "You think that's so fucking funny?" she screamed at me. "Well it's not." And then she burst into tears and slid down on the floor. "I really fell in love with him that night," she said. "And I can't find him! What if I never find him?"

I squeezed in and shut the door and locked it, then kneeled down next to her. "We're going to find him, Stella. I promise you. Actually, I promise you we'll look every-where. I assume you looked where you found him in the first place?"

She sniffled and nodded. "That place and every bar and restaurant in the area. And then I started scouring other neighborhoods." She threw up her hands.

"We'll find him," I told her again. "Come on back to the table. Rory's worried he offended you."

"Well he did," she said. "And so did you by laughing."

"We're both sorry," I told her, picking off a square of errant toilet paper from the back of her thigh.

At the table, Rory apologized again, and Stella dismissed it with a wave of her hands. "If we're fighting, we must be family," she said, smiling. She sipped her coffee and took a bite of her brownie. "Okay, let me ask you this, Rory. What would you do if you had this amazing connection with the one-night-stand chick, and then she…got pregnant and found you and told you. What would you do?"

"First of all, I just want to state for the record that I wouldn't get a girl pregnant on a one-night stand. I'd use a condom. But if it broke or something, I'd see the situation through. If she wanted to keep the baby, I'd support her. Financially and all ways. It's my kid, right?"

"Could you imagine falling in love with her?" Stella asked. "Someone you didn't know who was pregnant with your baby?"

"I don't know her because it was a one-night stand?"

Stella nodded. And waited.

He looked at her for a long minute, understanding dawning. "Yeah, I can imagine falling in love with her. If she was cool. Like you," he added, squeezing her hand and then excusing himself to the bathroom.

That seemed to make Stella feel better. She leaned back in her chair, gazing at the ceiling for a moment. "Isn't it strange that no one can tell? That at this very second, a baby is growing inside me, developing knees or fingernails or eyelashes and that no one even knows he or she is in there?"

I smiled. "Do you like that it's private? It won't be for long."

"I don't know. I feel so…responsible for it, you know? I'm the only one, Ruby. I'm all little Silas or Clarissa has."

"You have me," I said, patting her knee.

"And me," Rory said as he joined us again. "I know I seem like a cousin fifty times removed, but I'm technically a first cousin."

"You don't seem so removed," Stella said.

"Cool," Rory said, and it was.

Rory decided to stay put in Chicago. And Popper turned out okay. He lived in a skyscraper across from a giant stainless steel sculpture that looked like a bean. For twenty-two-year-olds, Rory and Popper were pretty mature. They took us out on the town, for deep-dish pizza, of course, and then to a jazz club where Popper said Norah Jones had once shown up and sang unannounced. She didn't that night.

I told Rory to call his mom and let her know he decided to hitch a ride with us to Popper's, where he was going to stay till he found his own place. He promised he would, told Stella she was going to make an excellent mother, and then we spent a half hour trying to figure out if Rory and the baby would be second cousins or first cousins once removed. We asked just about everyone in our path, but got different answers each time.

6

WE WERE ROBBED JUST OUTSIDE OF CEDAR RAPIDS, IOWA. Stella had spotted the words *Pie Diner*—something we thought only existed in the south—and insisted on stopping there for a late lunch. The place was a greasy spoon, but had a damned good hamburger, and six kinds of homemade pie. Stella thought it ridiculous that I ordered the apple pie when there were five more interesting varieties, but I loved apple pie. In her day, Grammy Zelda made a mean apple pie. Stella went for the s'mores pie; how was that any more interesting? When we got back into the car, which we'd had to park at the far end of the lot, Stella immediately noticed that her cup of malt balls was missing.

"My malt balls are gone," she said. "Oh shit, my makeup bag is gone! And my book!"

"Did you bring them into the diner with you?" I asked.

She shook her head. "Someone stole my stuff!"

I stared at her. "When we were walking from the car to the diner, I asked you if you locked the doors and you said yes, Stella."

"I thought I did."

I rolled my eyes and checked the trunk. Our suitcases were still there. There was a button inside the car that opened the trunk, so the thief clearly found our clothes worthless.

Thank God we'd both brought our purses; sometimes we just took some cash and left the purses in the trunk. In the supposedly locked car. The thought of having to cancel all my credit cards—not that I had more than two—and go to the DMV for a new license would have infuriated me. As would losing the wallet Tom had given me for my birthday last year, a tiny picture in a heart-shaped frame on my keychain of me, Stella and my mom, and the engagement card from Nick that had been addressed only to me. *Maybe we should be going there.*

I clutched my purse to my body.

"My prenatal vitamins were in my makeup bag," Stella said, kicking the tire. "And my forty-two-dollar moisturizer. Shit, shit, shit!"

"Who would steal someone's open container of malt balls?" I wondered aloud while Stella stopped someone getting out of his car to ask where the nearest police station was. And a stained, dog-eared copy of *What To Expect When*

You're Expecting, which you could find in every library, used bookstore or book bin at the town recycling center?

And who spent forty-two dollars on moisturizer?

The Isley, Iowa, police station happened to be around the corner. Talk about a brazen thief. The baby-faced cop in uniform who returned to the scene of the crime with us to check for evidence and clues said that crowded parking lot car burglaries were on the rise. From the sounds of what was stolen, he figured a down-on-her-luck pregnant lady saw Stella's malt balls and book and fancy makeup bag lying on the seat and couldn't resist trying the door and then taking the items.

"Probably in and out in fifteen seconds," the officer said. "In fact, I'd say she stole your property, then went into the pie diner for lunch. You were probably sitting a few feet from her.

There had been a pregnant woman a few tables away, as a matter of fact. Both Stella and I had noticed her come in because she was waddling and looked so uncomfortable in the early-July heat. She was alone, too. And had a tote bag. Which was probably hiding Stella's stuff.

"Maybe she's still inside," Stella said. "We can check her bag!"

"That would constitute an illegal search and seizure," the officer said. "Her pregnancy alone doesn't make her a suspect."

"Oh," Stella said. "I am never spending twenty-five bucks on mascara again."

"I can't comment on that one way or the other, ma'am," the officer said. "But I do suggest you lock your doors from here on in."

She declined to fill out a report. According to Stella, she'd rather spend the next hour in a drugstore buying all new Revlon or L'Oreal products than sitting in some hot police station.

As we drove away, Stella stopped short, then pulled over. "I was using the Denny's menu as a bookmark," she said. "In *What To Expect*." She burst into tears, leaning her face against the steering wheel.

I stared out the windshield. Numb. There was a reason I'd kept that stupid Denny's menu in my mother's hope chest. I'd always thought it was because my father's vows, on a kiddie menu, reminded me that he'd once loved my mother, that he'd once promised to love her forever and had meant it. I grew up believing that although he'd walked out, left her and us, taking his damned ten percent, that he'd once been good and true. The vows said so. I'd always accepted that people could change, for the better and worse, and Eric Miller had changed for the worse.

But now, thanks to Stella swiping the vows and using the menu as a bookmark, I had nothing to prove he'd once been better. And neither did Stella.

"He's out there somewhere, Ruby. Do you ever think about that? He's out there somewhere, eating scrambled eggs for breakfast, or taking a Tylenol for a headache or going to work or whatever. He's living and breathing somewhere right now."

"I don't know what you want me to say to that, Stella. How the hell can I care? He walked out on us. He left Mom and he left us and never looked back. Never sent a card, never tried to find us when we moved. He stopped being our father a long time ago. That man eating scrambled eggs isn't our dad, Stell."

"Except that he is."

Except that he is.

"I want the vows back," she said, her voice cracking.

"I know. Me, too. I'm the one who was hanging on to that Denny's menu, remember?"

She looked up at me. "I know."

"It's okay, Stella," I said, rubbing her back. "Maybe the universe is trying to tell us not to hang on to what *isn't*."

She sat back and let out a deep breath. "I have way too much of *what isn't* in my life, Ruby."

"Clarissa or Silas *is*," I told her, gently patting her belly. "I is, too."

She gave me a little smile and nodded and then started driving again.

The baby-faced cop had said we really couldn't drive through this area without stopping to see the scale-model of the USS Enterprise. Neither Stella nor I had known what he was talking about at first. But then we remembered someone in South Bend having mentioned it to Rory as a must-see. Apparently, the nearby town of Riverside was the future birthplace of Captain James T. Kirk (he would be born in Riverside on March 22, 2233). I'd never seen a single episode of *Star Trek*, but Tom was a huge fan of the show and had DVDs of all the movies, so how could I not get a picture of the minispaceship?

Besides, there was no way we could drive on to Nebraska. The five-hour drive from Chicago to Cedar Rapids had been long enough, and the loss of Stella's malt balls and the book and the vows had sent her into several crying jags. Somehow, the lack of malt balls symbolized the lack of Jake or James or Jason, the fruitlessness of finding the thief representing the fruitlessness of finding him. And the lost vows stood for the loss of her chance of a life with Jake or James or Jason.

So I called the hotel that Rory had booked us into in Lincoln and arranged for the room the following night. All the hotels we'd called in Riverside were booked, so we ended up at a tiny motel on the outskirts of town. In the small lot, we triple-checked that the car was locked up tight.

Inside the narrow four-story motel, *Star Trek* memorabilia filled every surface of every wall and table. At the front desk, Stella asked for a room with two queen-size beds, and the guy behind the counter—wearing Spock ears—said, "For God's sake, Jim, I'm a doctor—not the concierge of the Ritz!" Neither Stella nor I got it, so he explained, in detail, the inside joke from *Star Trek*, about how Bones constantly said, "For God's sake, Jim, I'm a doctor not a 'fill in the blank' when Captain Kirk would ask him to get creative in order to save them from oncoming aliens.

I was going to tell him that we had never seen a single episode of *Star Trek,* but that we had seen the first *Star Trek* movie, together, and liked it. I decided against that, though, since I was afraid that would land us in the "bad" room that every hotel had.

The room had lumpy twin beds but very strong air-conditioning, which we both felt was more important. We took showers, and while Stella primped with her toiletries, I called Tom. It was a short check-in conversation, all of thirty seconds long. I was exhausted from driving, and Tom had just gotten back from a six-mile run.

Stella turned from the mirror above the dresser and pointed her blush brush at me. "You know, if you didn't add the 'I love you, too,' before hanging up I would really wonder about you two."

"Meaning?" I asked in my most bored voice, dropping down on the bed. The pillow was soft and fluffy. I closed my eyes.

"Meaning, what kind of conversation was that? You just got engaged, but you might as well be an old boring married couple."

"There's nothing wrong with old, boring married couples, Stella. It's called being comfortable. It's called checking in. And that in itself is nice."

She stared at herself in the mirror. "I wish I had someone to check in with, actually."

"I didn't mean—"

"No, I know," she said, sweeping a sparkly sand shadow

across her eyelids. Who exactly was she primping for, anyway? "But still, I can't help but notice that you're not having long, romantic conversations with Tom every night."

Until just now, Tom and I hadn't spoken in a few days. Yesterday, I'd responded to his text message from the previous night with: *I'll call you when we get there. xo, R.* And he'd responded with *Ok. xo, T.* Which made me feel a little more comfortable. Suddenly I had room—to breathe, to think. If I wanted, if I really wanted, Tom would fly to Las Vegas and we would be married in a chapel just like that. If I wanted.

"We don't need to talk every day," I said.

She slicked on some lipstick, which was too bright for even her dramatic coloring, wiped it off and tried the other shade she'd bought, a pretty sheer rose. Then she flopped down on the bed, which squeaked, and put her arms behind her head. "I was just thinking about how Silas and I used to talk for like two hours every night on the telephone, even though we'd just spent hours together. We had so much to say to each other. It's been that way with every guy I've been in love with."

"Tom and I have a lot to say to each other."

"Then why aren't you saying it?" she asked. "Why didn't you tell him all about the burglary? Or about the incredible apple pie—you said it was the best pie you'd ever had in your life. You didn't even tell him about meeting Sally. Or our stowaway cousin. How could you not have been dying to tell him about all that?"

I took my own cosmetics bag from my suitcase, which

contained all of three beauty products: moisturizer (the four-dollar version), mascara and sheer lipstick. Other than that I had sunscreen with bug-spray protection, my trusty Secret antiperspirant, and a tiny vial of stick perfume (a delicious musk scent) that I got at Banana Republic. And that Nick always commented on.

I put on some mascara and lip gloss and played with my hair. "Maybe I'm just more private than you, Stella," I said, though that wasn't really true. "Did you ever think of that? Maybe I don't share my every thought and feeling."

"I never liked that about you," she said.

Which made me laugh. A few times when we were growing up, Stella would literally grab me by the shoulders and say, "Tell me what you are thinking, dammit!"

Tom and I did have a lot to say to each other. We just chose not to discuss everything to death. I could talk about love with Tom, or politics, or family, or our wedding, or teaching, or school gossip, anything. But most of the time, I just enjoyed having him there. Even when I had a rush of things to say to Tom, his presence was so calming, so sturdy, that I sometimes felt that rush steady itself.

A friend at BLA once vented to me that her boyfriend never talked to her, that when she tried to talk to him about how they never talked, he'd say he was content to be in the same room with her and didn't need to make small talk. She would rant how she wasn't talking about small talk, that she wanted a real conversation, but he insisted if you had to make real conversation, you were really making small talk.

Because you had to think about it, he insisted, and therefore it wasn't real.

They broke up a few dates later. My friend had told me I was lucky that I "thought like a guy," that it was no wonder Tom and I had such a good relationship. I tried to tell her that I had no idea how men thought, that Tom and I were simply compatible, but she didn't buy it.

Stella got up and stood next to me in front of the mirror, scooping up her long hair and twisting it into a bun at the nape of her neck. "I hope J and I have a lot to say when I find him. I mean, I know we'll have a lot to say, given what I have to tell him. But I mean after that, after the shock wears off, when it's just two people together. We had so much to say the night we met. We talked for hours about everything and nothing. But what if it was just the booze? What if he turns out to be a total stranger?"

I looked at her reflection. "Well, Stella, he will be, really. But you have something very big in common now. You'll need to develop your relationship based on that."

Now *that* would be a challenge. Though I supposed the *New York Times* article and question fifteen didn't apply to Stella (not that she was getting married) or those who were starting at square two or three. There *was* no strength of the relationship to *be* challenged. They were starting with the challenge. *They* were the challenge.

I told her about the article, about how she was my challenge to question fifteen.

She laughed. "I'm not the challenge, Ruby. The *truth* is.

I'm just the one bringing it up, making you really think about what you're doing, what you want."

"I wouldn't have said yes if I didn't want to marry Tom," I pointed out. Miss Defensive.

"Yes, you would have," she said. "People say yes to things all the time for the wrong reasons, or for the right reasons for the wrong situation."

"So I shouldn't marry a man I love, a man I've been with for over two years, a man who has stood by me through thick and thin, but you should go off into the sunset with a total stranger?"

"He's not a stranger," she answered in a singsongy voice. "He's the father of your niece or nephew."

I held her gaze in the mirror. "I hope things work out with him. I hope he's open to you, to the baby, to working out your problems—"

"If we have any," she interrupted. "Maybe it'll be true love. Maybe he'll be thrilled about the baby."

"Are you?" I asked. It was the question she'd refused to answer so far.

She took a deep breath. "I was scared at first, but now I *am* thrilled. Maybe he will be, too. I think if two people want the relationship bad enough, if you really, really love each other, then you make it work." She stared at herself, then used her index finger to rub off some of her eyeshadow. "So what are some of the questions from the article?"

"Everything from how you're going to handle money to whether you can stand each other's families."

"Those are big deals?" she said. "They sound pretty minor to me."

"Fights and resentment over seemingly small things can lead to divorce."

"So can big tits," Stella pointed out. "Our father left for a hot young body and his freedom, not because of all that other stuff."

"But agreeing on fundamentals must make things easier," I said. "Like if Tom wants four kids and I want one, we should decide before we get married so that when we're ready to have kids, there are no surprises."

"But either of you could change your mind at any point," she said. "Let's say Tom told you he wanted the mother of his children to stay at home and not work. You would probably tell him to quit *his* job. But when you actually had a kid, you might *want* to be a stay-at-home mom. How can you really decide anything before you're *there?*"

She had a point, but… I had no idea what the *but* was exactly. I just knew it was important to work things out, to be clear about how you felt, where you stood on important issues.

Right now, I needed to be figuring out where I stood on Nick McDermott, but if I were honest, I was…afraid to. Afraid to wonder. I glanced at my ring, and as usual, its sturdy sparkle gave me comfort.

The desk clerk recommended a bar and grill two blocks up called Spock Block that had good salads (according to his girlfriend), bad burgers (too gristly, according to his mother and aunt) and decent fish and chips (per him), which was what I was in the mood for. Stella had a craving for even bad French onion soup, and he assured us that they had that.

I was expecting the inside of the restaurant to be like inside the USS Enterprise, but aside from all the waitstaff wearing their pointy Vulcan Spock ears, it was just your average bar and grill.

The moment the hostess led us from the tiny waiting area into the main dining room, the restaurant got very quiet. As in a real hush fell over the crowd.

"Do you think they all saw the *Where Are They Now?* show?" she whispered, suddenly glowing and smoothing her hair.

"I think *that's* what has their attention," I said, gesturing in the direction of the guy on one knee in front of a girl's chair.

There were murmurs of "aww" and "how sweet!" but the couple looked frighteningly young. They couldn't be older than sixteen. Seventeen tops. They were both skinny, the same height, around five-nine, and had the same platinum-colored hair. His was short with a poof in the front. Hers was long and wildly curly, a little orange flower tucked in front of her ear. They both wore skinny black pants and black shirts—his a T-shirt, hers a tight tank top with the number 8 in white on her chest.

The guy placed his hand over his heart, a ring nowhere

in sight. "Vanessa, I love you like the sky loves the bird. Will you marry me?"

"Omigod, yes, Vincent!" she shrieked and flew into his arms, knocking him to the floor, where they kissed like mad. "Yes, yes, yes!" she said between breathy moans.

Their audience clapped and cheered and whistled.

"I wish I had a ring," he said between his own breathy moans.

She glanced at her hands, pulled off a silver ring from her right thumb and handed it to him.

"With this ring, I thee engage," he said and slid it down her finger, then they started making out again.

The waiters and a few other patrons kept clapping, so Stella and I did, too. I wondered if this was all some kind of *Star Trek* reenactment, but the couple didn't look like space creatures and weren't wearing Spock ears. Still, they were teenagers!

"Congratulations!" Stella said to them as they sat back down. "Ruby, my sister," she added, gesturing at me across the table, "just got engaged two weeks ago."

"Congrats to you, too," Vanessa said. "Your ring is so gorgeous." She glanced at her new fiancé. "Not that I don't love mine," she said quickly. "I don't need a ring to symbolize our commitment." Which led to the kissing of each other's hands.

A comical cough—four, actually, before it was heard by the lovebirds—announced that their dinner had arrived, so they parted for their individual seats, clutching hands across the table. They linked arms a lot, making a mess on the table with spilled soup.

"So I assume that's how you and Tom were when you got engaged, right?" Stella asked, eyes on the menu. "All kissy pooh and lovey-dovey, right? Oh, wait. I keep forgetting that he proposed in school."

"We're not sixteen," I whispered.

"We're *eighteen,*" the girl informed us.

I felt my cheeks burn. "I didn't mean—"

Vanessa rolled her eyes. "Yes, you did. *Everyone* thinks we're too young to be so serious, but we know how we feel, so everyone else can MYOB. Right?" she said to her beloved.

"Righto," he said. "That means *mind your own business,*" he added to us, eyeing us skeptically. The BLA kids spoke to each other in acronyms all day long. I was well versed in obnoxious.

"That's my answer to you, too, Stella," I told her. "MYOB."

"Whatev," was her retort. The waiter came over, and Stella asked for a taste of the onion soup. When he returned with a teeny cupful of it, her face lit up with one spoonful. She ordered two bowls and a house salad with cherry tomatoes, which they didn't have. I went for the fish and chips.

She handed her menu back to the waiter and turned her attention to me. "So they shouldn't get married because they're too young, but you should get married even though you don't love your fiancé?"

"Omigod, you're marrying someone you don't love?" Vanessa asked. "He's rich, right?"

"He's a schoolteacher," I said, glaring at my sister.

"Oh. So he's poor *and* you don't love him?" Vanessa said. "And you're marrying him because…"

"Because I *do* love him. Stella here thinks I don't. But she's wrong. She's also not me, but seems to think she knows how I feel."

"I am a highly respected face reader," Stella said. "And your face tells me all I need to know. Just because you agree on how to live your life doesn't mean you love each other. 'Ooh, we both like spending Sundays with your mother, Tom! Ooh, we both like watching *The Tonight Show* before bed! Ooh, we both like saving money and sex twice a month!' That's not love, Ruby. It's just compatibility."

"Duh," Vanessa said. "What do you think makes a relationship work? If Vincent and I weren't compatible, we wouldn't be in love in the first place. I mean, can you see me with some dorky guy in a plaid shirt and bad hair?"

"You make very good points, Vanessa," Stella said. "But some people may choose compatibility and safety of choice over love. Some may think love is compatibility, when it's being with someone who makes your heart move."

I thought of Nick and tried to replace his face, his body, with Tom. It didn't happen. It was those dark eyes, that unpredictability, that passion of Nick's that so often did literally make my heart lurch in my chest. "But you can be madly in love with someone, Stella, and not be compatible, not be able to live with that person."

Vincent shook his head. "That makes, like, zero sense. I

mean, that person must have what you want if you fell in love in the first place."

"Yeah, Ruby. That makes, like, zero sense," Stella said, grinning.

I rolled my eyes. "Hey, face reader, is my expression telling you that I wish an evil genie would come along and zip your mouth?"

"What *I* wish is that I could have ordered a Caesar salad, but according to the book you got me—and now we have to get another one—I can't eat raw eggs."

"I read about that, too. I was going to get a Caesar, but in honor of you, I didn't."

Stella raised her glass at me. "That's sisterhood."

"Wow, you *are* sisters," Vanessa said. "My older sister and I always fight like crazy, and then like a minute later, she's like, can I borrow your pink tank top, and I'm like, okay, and then we're best friends again."

"You can borrow my Hot Mama tank if you want," Stella said, smiling at me. "Ew, which reminds me—did you hear that baby-faced cop call me *ma'am?* I'm not even thirty yet! I've got weeks to go. Why would he call me *ma'am?*"

"I would call you *ma'am,*" Vincent commented around a mouthful of something orange.

"I guess that forty-dollar moisturizer really wasn't working," I said, and she laughed.

As our waiter cleared our plates and then took our dessert orders, the happy couple were back on each other's laps, feeding each other Mississippi Mud Cake that the waiter announced was on the house.

"I secretly read her face," Stella told me as she sipped her decaf. "The joy looks true-blue. His, too."

"Because they're babies!" I insisted. "They don't know what they're doing."

"Ruby, they're engaged. Not running off to Las Vegas to get married. And why are you worrying about people you don't even know?"

I glanced at V Squared, as Stella had started calling them, and decided to put them out of my mind. A moment later, that proved impossible as from out of nowhere, a DJ announced it was karaoke time, and V Squared squealed and leapt up and ran to the makeshift stage by the door, where a karaoke machine, a microphone and two stools had been set up.

Vanessa and Vincent turned out to be Elvis Presley fans. They sang "Love Me Tender," "Hound Dog" and "I Can't Help Falling in Love," for which they got a standing ovation from the small crowd that had gathered in Spock Block. Apparently, at eight o'clock every night, Spock Block turned into a karaoke joint.

"Do another!" someone shouted, and I had to agree that Vincent and Vanessa were good. They had a country twang, incongruent to their look and bad attitude, but they were both good singers and clearly loved to perform. For their encore, they did "Suspicious Minds."

It took Stella over ten minutes and a promise to drive the

first leg tomorrow morning if I did just one duet with her. I reminded her that I couldn't sing—and that neither could she—but she said the baby would get a kick out of it—literally (padumpa!)—and I finally relented. She chose "We Are Family" by Sister Sledge, which got me all mushy, and that was how I found myself singing on a tiny stage in a restaurant in Riverside, Iowa.

"Shake it!" Vanessa called out, but I drew the line at shaking it. When we got back to our table, she said, "You weren't half-bad. We've been doing the karaoke circuit on our way to Nashville. We've even won a couple of contests. We bill ourselves as the Singing Teen Elvis Lovebirds. People love it. We can sing anything, though. Rock, alternative, country, whatever. Maybe not metal. We don't have the screech."

The Singing Teen Elvis Lovebirds turned out to be from Minneapolis, had just graduated from high school, and were rebelling against their authoritarian parents who were insisting the pair go to college or get jobs and not fritter away their lives on singing or unattainable dreams.

"Like they're not glued to *American Idol* three times a week when it's on," Vincent said, rolling his eyes. "That show is total proof that a good singer can make it—if you put yourself out there."

Vanessa nodded. "Can you imagine really, really, really wanting something, and seeing a way to get it, but not going for it? I mean, you might as well be dead."

Nick McDermott's face floated into my mind again. His

body, too. He wore those army-green cargos he liked, and his black Converse sneakers, and no shirt. He smelled like Nick. He was telling me about a revelation he'd had while rereading *Billy Budd,* and how he was going to teach it differently.

But I'm talking about the real thing. Ever since you got engaged, I can't stop thinking about you. About us, Ruby. About the what-if, you know?

But then my cell rang, and it was Tom, and Nick's image—*poof*—disappeared. I headed over to the little foyer by the restrooms, but it was still too loud in the place, and I could barely catch Tom saying he couldn't hear me and would call tomorrow. I did hear his *I love you,* though, and I wasn't even sure he said it.

7

THE NEXT MORNING, SHEETS OF RAIN POURED DOWN FROM THE gray sky. I could barely see out the windshield, even with the windshield wipers swishing like crazy. Stella was supposed to drive this morning, but she couldn't drive straight when the weather was crystal clear.

"Let's just wait it out," she said, pouring her new container of malt balls into a cup in the holder between us. Last night, after saying goodbye and good luck to the V Squared, we'd gone to four different convenience stores, drugstores and supermarkets to find Stella's addiction. No luck. But after we'd snapped a few photographs of the USS Enterprise for Tom, hoping they wouldn't be too dark, Stella had had the brilliant idea to check a movie theater. She bought ten containers.

We'd both vowed to eat better from here on in, for ourselves and for Silas or Clarissa. To make up for the malt balls, which she couldn't and wouldn't give up, she promised to eat twice as many vegetables and fruits. Our motel had set up a continental breakfast in the little lobby, so we'd helped ourselves to bran muffins and fruit and read the local paper. I had to hand it to Stella for giving up caffeine so completely and without complaint. I *needed* my morning coffee.

She'd been impressing me since we left Maine. Yesterday, as we'd left the motel for dinner at Spock Block, she'd asked the desk clerk for the name and number of the nearest pharmacy, then called her OB's service and left a message asking them to call her in a new prescription for her stolen prenatal vitamins first thing in the morning. After breakfast, she walked the few blocks to pick it up. The twin sister who never seemed to care much about anything cared very much about the baby.

When the rain let up enough for me to at least see street signs, we took off, but stopped a few blocks up at the sight of two familiar flashes of platinum-blond hair at the corner. And two upturned thumbs.

"Oh, God, is that Vincent and Vanessa?" I said, squinting at the windshield. "Hitchhiking?"

Stella peered, too. "We'd better give them a ride. They are definitely too stupid to live."

"I hate that expression."

"But they are," she responded, malt ball in her cheek. "If we don't pick them up, who knows whose car they'll get into. Vanessa will be sold into sex slavery and Vincent will be found wrapped in plastic bags in some river."

I grimaced at her, pulled over in front of the singing teenaged lovebirds, and rolled down the windows. "I thought you were hanging out here for a while and then you were catching a bus or train for Nashville."

"We really, really talked last night," Vanessa said, adjusting the wet newspaper on her head. "We don't want to wait to get married. Once our parents hear we're engaged, they'll totally try to talk us out of it. So we're going to Las Vegas! To an Elvis wedding chapel! Did you know that an Elvis impersonator will not only officiate, but serenade you after the ceremony? I totally want to get that on videotape." She turned to Vincent, who stood dripping wet next to her, no newspaper on his platinum-blond head. No poof, either. "Who'll videotape, though? It'll just be us. No friends, no family." She gnawed her lip.

"The employees will act as witnesses," I said. "So, someone will film the ceremony if you want."

"If we *pay* for it," Vincent said.

"Don't worry!" she snapped at him. "We'll earn a fortune on the karaoke contest circuit. We'll pay our way down and have enough for an amazing hotel room, too."

"Why didn't you just ask us for a ride?" I said. "You could have just knocked on our door this morning."

"Honestly?" Vanessa said. "We weren't sure we'd want to spend that long in a car with you two."

Stella threw a malt ball at her.

Vincent turned on his hundred-watt smile. "But since we're headed the same way and no one's stopped for us, can we hitch a ride?"

"How are you going to help pay for gas?" Stella asked in her best smug voice.

"We'll sing for you," Vanessa said in all earnestness.

"Hop in," I told them. They both sagged with relief, threw their duffel bags in the trunk, and got in the backseat.

And sing they did. Elvis songs we'd never heard before. Then Vincent broke out with *Bridge Over Troubled Water* and a Marilyn Manson song to show his range. Vanessa sang Carrie Underwood, her idol. Then they both slept, mouths open, in the backseat for close to forty-five minutes, until the loudest wail of a fire truck siren woke them up.

I thought about telling them of our brief brush with fame, but there seemed little point. Vincent's stomach audibly growled, so we stopped for lunch at a cute place called Attack of the Killer Salad.

We lined up to choose our greens and mix-ins and dressings. Vincent asked the woman behind the counter if there was a discount for choosing fewer than the six add-ins you got for six dollars and ninety-nine cents. I assured him that lunch was on me, and he asked for grilled salmon in his salad, which was extra. Vanessa wanted shrimp. Grifters.

"So are you two going to pick stage names? Like Shania Twain?" Stella asked as we sat down with our trays at a booth.

"Twain isn't a stage name," Vanessa said, spearing a cucumber. "It was her stepfather's last name. She renamed herself Shania from Eileen. But she had to do that. I mean, how many Eileens have become superstars?"

"How many Shanias have?" Stella asked.

"Yeah, but Shania is original and cool," Vincent said. "It has cred."

My mother once told me and Stella that when the jobs stopped coming in, our father had wanted to change our names and market us as adorable "fresh" six-year-olds, but my mother had refused. We were Ruby and Stella Miller, and if that wasn't good enough for the agencies, too bad. According to my mother, Eric Miller had said it *was* too bad and that she didn't know a whit about the entertainment industry or how it worked. If we had changed our names, I often wondered what our father would call us at home. By the new name or the old?

"Anyway, we already have stage names," Vincent said, popping a crouton into his mouth. "My *given* name is Andrew, but forget that totalitarian bullshit. Just because I was named after my father doesn't mean I have to carry that albatross on my back."

The teacher in me yearned to say something about his mixed metaphors, but at least he was using them.

"Is your name really Vanessa?" I asked his female half.

"In my soul it is," she said. "But my birth certificate says Kathryn. With a *K*. And an *R-Y-N*. If you're going to name your kid that, why not go for the real thing, *Catherine,* the way it was meant to be spelled. The *Jane Eyre* way."

"*Wuthering Heights,*" I corrected.

She thought about that for a minute. "Oh, that's right. *Wuthering Heights.* With Heathcliff. Omigod, Vincent, maybe we should go by Catherine and Heathcliff instead of Vanessa and Vincent. I could call you Heath."

"Isn't that, like, a candy bar?" he asked. "I like Vincent better."

"Fine," she said. "Vincent. It's very artisty, anyway."

"I think you should call yourselves V Squared," Stella said.

Vincent stared at her as though she had an extra head. "That doesn't sound very country. We're going to be known as Vincent and Vanessa."

That didn't sound very country, either, but as a former New Yorker and Mainer, what did I know about such things?

"Stella once changed her name for an entire summer," I said. "At sleepaway camp. Only the camp staff and I knew that her name wasn't really Hermione."

Vanessa snorted. "That's so lame. Let me guess, you just read *Harry Potter* or something."

"Or something," Stella retorted with a dirty look. She smiled. "Actually you're right. And I'm proud of it, bitch."

Vanessa was shocked for a split second before she realized Stella was kidding. About the *bitch*. She burst out laughing. "Omigod, I love you guys."

Good thing, because we had twenty-one hours of traveling left.

Somewhere between Des Moines and the Nebraska border in Omaha, Vincent and Vanessa moved to opposite ends of the backseat. They sat with their arms crossed over their chests, both staring out their respective windows. Every now and then, Vanessa would fiddle with her ring.

Stella had told them about the list of questions that couples should ask before getting married, and most of them, which I had to struggle to remember, V Squared dismissed with snorts and grimaces (would they have kids and who would take care of said kids) or *Oh, please, who cares?* (ways in which their families bugged them), and *Who gave a rat's ass* (the division of household chores). As for discussing financial goals and spending habits, their answer was: *What money?* They'd never discussed their health histories, yet did so in the car. Family health issues included cancer, agoraphobia and tonsil-lectomies. They started making out to the question about whether or not each was affectionate to the degree the other wanted, and unfortunately demonstrated their answer to how comfortable they were talking about their sexual desires.

They both wanted a television in the bedroom. They both grew up attending the same Congregational church and liked God and thought it was retro-cool to go to church every Sunday.

One question tripped them up. (And it wasn't number fifteen.)

"Wait a minute," Vanessa said. "You *actually* think you listen to me? You actually think you consider the stuff I say and complain about?"

"Well, c'mon, Kath, you know you make a big deal out of everything." He rolled his eyes in our direction.

"First of all, it's *Vanessa*," she snapped. "And second of all, excuse me?" This was when she started inching over toward the window.

"Yeah, but who you really are is Kathryn. And Kathryn stresses about everything. Just because you changed your name doesn't mean you're not the same person."

"That's deep, *Andrew*," she said, crossing her arms over her chest.

Stella turned around to face them. "So do you two think the bond between you can survive this little argument?" she asked a little too gleefully.

"I'm not speaking to him at the moment," Vanessa said.

Vincent rolled his eyes. "See what I mean?" he said to Stella.

"What are the other questions?" Vanessa asked. "I think *Andrew* and I should definitely make sure our answers mesh."

"There was one about friends," I said. "If you respect the other's friends, like them, etc."

Vanessa snorted. "His friends are morons."

"Your friends are stupid sluts," Vincent retorted.

"Stop this car!" Vanessa said. "Stop this car right now."

"Vanessa," I said, "it's getting dark, and I want to be in Lincoln before I have trouble reading the street signs. I think you two should discuss these questions like adults. If you are adults. Because only adults should get married."

"Preachy," Vanessa muttered.

"Okay, Samantha isn't a stupid slut," Vincent said.

"Why, because she would sleep with you when she was your girlfriend?"

"Ooh, you used to date Vanessa's friend?" Stella asked. "That's tough."

"I didn't love her," Vincent snapped at me. "So it doesn't matter."

"Really?" Vanessa asked, inching closer. "You didn't?"

"I've only ever loved you," he said. Which prompted another long make out session, hands roving everywhere, *I am so sorry I said that* amid their breathy moans and *I love you so much*.

"There's just one more we didn't cover," I said. "About whether or not there's anything you will *not* give up in the marriage."

"Like a deal breaker?" Vincent said, glancing at Vanessa.

I nodded. "A deal breaker."

"Neither of us wants to ever go back to Minnesota, so that totally takes care of all the questions about our families getting up our butts. That stuff probably causes more problems for couples than anything."

He finally had a good point.

Luckily for us, the lovebirds got into another huge fight at a gas station in Omaha.

They decided to "hang there" and live among the plains, maybe take a bus or train up to the famous Highway 12 and ride along the Outlaw Trail, where Jesse James and his gang hid among the deep canyons and brush cover. According to Vincent, God would shepherd them to Las Vegas when it was the right time, then over to Nashville and make them stars. They wouldn't forget our hospitality and, oh, yeah, could they borrow fifty bucks? They'd pay us back and then some with the payout from their first gig.

Oh, and if I had the URL for the *New York Times* article, they'd appreciate it.

8

THE HOTEL THAT RORY BOOKED FOR US IN LINCOLN, NEBRASKA, was not only called The Double Sisters Inn, but our stay had been prepaid. Stella insisted it was karma. For our generosity to V Squared of fifty bucks, a few meals and a long hard look at their relationship, we now could splurge on a very expensive dinner.

But the very best part was that Rory had paid for two rooms! Which meant I finally had a break from Stella. I would not have to listen to her snore for an entire night. The moment I was alone in my room (the sign above the door dubbed it The Peaceful Room), I called Rory to thank him, but got his machine and left an effusive message. I owed him one.

In fifteen minutes, Stella and I were expected by the proprietors, two women in their fifties, for "the quiet hour" in the parlor, so I had only fifteen minutes to flop on my bed and breathe deeply. The room was so lovely! The walls were the palest salmon and the furnishings a warm wood. Fresh flowers were on the old-fashioned bureau, and a round rug of faded cabbage roses decorated the wide-planked wood floors in front of the bed. And the bed was so grand—four-poster with a gauzy canopy and down-filled pillows.

I forced myself off the bed, did a quick freshening up in the tiny private bathroom, and knocked on Stella's door, but she must have already left. In the Victorian-style parlor, I found her sitting on the love seat by the bay window. The proprietors hovered over her with a large box of tea to choose from.

"Delightful!" Maxine said. "Ruby is here as well."

After we chose our teas, the two women hurried off to the kitchen and quickly returned, one holding a tray containing pots of tea and cream and sugar, the other holding a tray of tiny sandwiches and plates of cookies.

This was heaven.

The women sat across from us on a matching love seat and told us all about themselves. They were Charlotte and Maxine Holcomb, also fraternal twins. (And they were thrilled to hear that Stella and I were as well.) The sisters looked almost identical and had the same style, which Stella would refer to as Hippie Dippie. Meaning long hair (in this case, an ash-brown with streaks of gray), long skirts (gauze and earth-toned), long necklaces (and many, from colorful beads to pendants, including a Jewish star and a cross), long earrings (one wore feathers, the other tiny pugs), no makeup (and good skin), and a sense of both serenity and joy. They'd married brothers (not twins) in a double wedding ceremony and had been happily married for almost twenty-five years.

Maxine was telling us about the history of The Double Sisters, which was located out in the country, but a short drive to downtown and the varied neighborhoods. She and Charlotte had grown up smack in the middle of Nebraska, in a town with a population of eighty-six. They'd dreamed of moving to Lincoln, the big city, and starting a dress shop, which they did and still owned, and then they decided to start a bed-and-breakfast that would cater to small-towners like they'd been and make them feel welcome and safe and cared for. So the two sets of siblings decided to invest in the antique farmhouse with its gorgeous gardens and start a business. The husbands were both in-demand carpenters and craftsmen, and their skills showed in every room.

Stella and I had once talked about opening a bed-and-breakfast in Blueberry Hills, the town our mother loved so much. Blueberry was semi-famous for its annual summer (you guessed it—blueberry) festival in August, with its carnival and craft show and buckets upon buckets of blueberries. The festival attracted a good crowd, and area inns and motels were always booked for that weekend. When our mother died, we thought we'd honor her by opening our own inn, something she'd often talked about, but when we sat down with a book about opening an inn, we quickly discovered the expense and management of running a bed-and-breakfast would prove beyond us. Besides, Stella had decided she couldn't live in Maine, couldn't give up New York, until she was at least eighty.

"Congratulations, dear!" Maxine suddenly said, and I realized she was looking at my ring. "When is the big day?"

"We haven't set a date," I said, taking a bite of a tiny chicken salad sandwich.

"Because she's still deciding if she should marry him," Stella announced. "She's not sure."

"Stella!" I snapped around my food. How dared she? It was one thing to voice her opinions to me—or "kid" to Rory or the engaged teenagers, who needed a discussion about marriage, but it was quite another to the proprietors of our bed-and-breakfast.

"That's quite common," Charlotte said, smiling gently at me. "It could be a case of cold feet, or a case of the brains, or a case of the just-not-readies."

"Which is it, dear?" Maxine asked, holding out the plate of cookies.

I took a raspberry-filled butter cookie. "The only one who isn't sure if I should marry Tom is you, Stella," I said, shooting her a glare. "I'm *quite* sure."

Because Tom was safe? Because he would never leave me? Because I could count on him forever? Were those the reasons why I loved him? Did I not love him for him? But those reasons *were* Tom. So how in the world could you differentiate?

The sisters smiled at us and munched on their cookies. "It's a good thing we were sure we were dating the wrong brothers," Charlotte said. "Can you imagine if I married William? We would have killed each other before our first anniversary!"

Stella and I stared at each other. "You switched husbands?" I asked.

"Well, they weren't our husbands then," Maxine said, pouring a cup of tea for herself. "We switched boyfriends. Oh, it's such fun to remember! I was dating CJ, and Charlotte was dating William, but I thought William was so handsome, and Charlotte loved how quiet CJ was, and how his silences drove me bananas! So we pulled the ole twin switch on a double date to find out if we might really like the other guy better. Now mind you, this was when we'd only been out a few times, so they weren't able to tell us apart."

I laughed. "Did you tell them the night that you switched?"

Maxine smiled. "We came clean the next day, after Charlotte and I had talked it over. We had no idea how they'd react. I mean, just because we look alike doesn't mean we are alike necessarily. The boys might have liked their original girls. But it turned out they were happy with the switch, too."

"CJ couldn't stand Maxine's laugh," Charlotte said playfully. "He thought she laughed too loud and talked too loud and too much. He still thinks so."

That earned Charlotte a gentle nudge in the ribs from Maxine. "And William thought Charlotte was way too full of herself, all high-and-mighty."

"I am and rightly so," Charlotte said, and both sisters dissolved in laughter. It was clear why CJ didn't want to listen to Maxine laugh for the rest of her life. She had the Janice-from-*Friends* laugh. But louder, and slower.

"But how did you know the other brother was The One?" I asked. "I understand how you knew the original guy wasn't."

"I think you know someone is The One when you want to say yes, heart, mind, and soul," Maxine said.

"Do you want to say yes to Tom heart, mind, and soul?" Stella asked, her eyes in Face Reader concentration. I'd seen her adopt that look enough times to know she was getting ready to give me her own personal lie-detector test.

"Yes," I said in all truthfulness. If she'd added "and body," I might have had to say no.

I lay in a lavender-scented bubble bath in a white clawfoot tub, a row of tea candles along the edge of the wall, and a refreshing glass of lemon-water in reach-distance. I'd never been to a spa, but now I understood why women went. When I got back home, I'd have to re-create this in my bathroom, complete with thick, soft pale-green towels and a cuddly terry robe and matching slippers. A variety of bath lotions also awaited my exit from the tub, but I planned to stay in for hours. My plan was to just lay there and think. About Tom. About Nick. About pink bridesmaid dresses. About getting married in Las Vegas. About not.

My cell phone rang. Nick.

"Um, could you just hang on for a moment," I asked him. "I'm just getting out of a bubble bath."

I wondered if he was picturing me naked. Given how he said he felt about me, I assumed he was. But I'd always felt so...*not* undressed by Nick McDermott's eyes. I always felt asexual around him, that I wasn't the type of woman who'd interest McDreamy. The way Sonia Flores, our Spanish teacher, or Jennifer Tarp (Latin) or Christine Calverton (social studies) did. These women all had one thing in common: playboy-bunny figures and breathy voices. Jennifer wasn't particularly pretty, but that body! And she had a Marilyn Monroe voice that seemed utterly incongruent for the teaching of Latin, but which transfixed men. Including Nick. They'd dated for two weeks, and then Jennifer began arriving at school in a bad mood for a couple of weeks.

I put on the robe and slippers and padded into my room and flopped down on my back on the bed.

"Hi," I said.

"Where are you?" he asked.

"In an adorable bed-and-breakfast in Lincoln, Nebraska. And it's called The Double Sisters Inn—isn't that amazing? My cousin, Rory—I have to tell you all about him and how we met—he booked me and Stella here, and paid in advance for two separate rooms, and you should see the clawfoot tub—"

"I'll be there by midnight," he said. "If I can get a flight that leaves right away."

I sat up. "What?"

"I've always wanted to see Nebraska. The Oregon trail. Isn't that where Jesse James and his gang hid?"

"That's way up north," I said. "Lincoln is actually—"

"I don't really want to see Nebraska, Ruby. I want to see *you*. I need to talk to you, face-to-face."

"So you're really going to fly out here? Right now?"

"Isn't that what Saturdays are for? See you soon," he said.

I knocked on Stella's door. She was curled up in the peach chair next to the window, reading *The Girlfriends' Guide to Pregnancy,* which she'd bought during her brief exploration of downtown Lincoln. While I'd been in deep relaxation in the tub, Stella had done some serious shopping. This included buying two dresses at Maxine and Charlotte's dress shop, one for her and one for me. Same dress in different colors that, according to Maxine, matched our color palette. Apparently, I was a summer and should never wear black. Stella was a winter, and therefore looked stunning in black. Our dresses were cotton and sleeveless and to the knee, with a row of gingham at the empire waist. Stella's was white and mine a pale pink. We both already had several flip-flops to match.

Do not tell Stella about Nick. Do not tell Stella about Nick. Do not tell Stella about Nick.

I paced in front of the window, toyed with the velvet pink drapery and tucked my hair behind my ears over and over.

"Ruby, what the hell is wrong with you?" Stella asked, staring at me.

"Nothing," I said. "Nothing. Why would anything be wrong? Nothing's wrong. Nothing!" I tucked my hair behind my ears again, but it wouldn't stay and I slid down onto the floor onto my butt.

Stella peered over the bed at me. "Okay, I'm sorry about what I said before. I'm sorry for everything I've ever done. But doesn't the dress I bought for you make up for—"

"Nick is coming here. He's on a plane right now. Well, he's on his way to the airport right now."

"Nick?" she repeated. "The hot teacher?"

I shot up and resumed pacing, toying with the drapes, fiddling with my hair. I repeated my mantra not to tell her, and then told her everything.

Her mouth dropped open. "Talk about a grand gesture! Ruby, don't you see? Even the universe is telling you not to marry Tom Truby. Not to be Ruby Truby."

"I'm scared," I whispered, sitting down on her bed. "He's coming here, Stella. I won't cheat on Tom. I won't do that."

"Is kissing Nick cheating?" she asked. "I don't think it is."

"Actually, I think it is. An emotional affair is no different than a sexual affair. In fact, an emotional affair might be worse, because the heart is involved."

She raised an eyebrow. "So you're going to not kiss—or sleep with—the guy of your dreams, of your every fantasy, the guy who's telling you he wants a chance with you, so that you can not cheat on your dull fiancé, who you don't love and shouldn't marry?"

I stood up and walked back to the windows, staring out at the row of trees. I would not be able to convince Stella that I did love Tom. But the thing was, I did.

Then why didn't I call him every night? Why didn't I rush to tell him all about Rory? About the inn? About the burglary? About the mini USS Enterprise? Why did I want to tell Nick everything, but not Tom?

Tom was willing to fly to Las Vegas to marry me in a drive-through chapel, and I…wasn't. Yet, anyway.

"Well, the good news for you, Ruby, is that he's en route. So whatever happens is out of your hands."

"Of course it's in my hands," I said. "I control what happens to me."

She rolled her eyes. "Ruby, you should think with your heart more. Less with your head."

"My heart says Nick is a womanizer. That I'll destroy my relationship with Tom for a couple of weeks, a couple of tortured months with a guy who'll break my heart."

"You don't know he'll break your heart."

"Yes, I do, Stell. He's not interested in a relationship. Or he's incapable."

"Or he hasn't met the right woman."

I shook my head. "I'm sure the right woman has come

and gone several times and he wasn't willing to get serious, or he got distracted by the next hot babe."

"Then it hasn't been the right time," Stella said. "The right person stops you dead in your tracks."

"It's never been the right time for Nick. I find that suspicious."

"Lemme ask you something," she said. "If Tom hadn't proposed, would you be hoping he would?"

No. Not yet, anyway.

"Your lack of answer means no."

I shrugged. "We live together. I know he's committed to me, to the relationship. I've always known we would get married."

She stared at me. "I'm just trying to imagine going for a guy like Tom in the first place when there's a guy like Nick at work every day. I mean, how could you stand it? You kiss Blah goodbye in the dorky school office and then you see Nick walking around. How can you bear to kiss Tom after even looking at Nick?"

"First of all, Tom is perfectly attractive. Second of all, there's nothing wrong with a harmless fantasy crush."

My mother once told me that she had a huge crush on the actor Sean Connery and that she'd gone to see all his Bond films and every one of his action movies with my father just so she could stare at Sean for two hours. And when the credits rolled and the lights came on and my mother went from gazing upon Sean Connery to her own husband, she said the feeling was the same. No momentary pang of disappointment, of reality settling in. She was as hot for her everyday husband as she was for a man once named *People*'s Sexiest Man Alive. She rarely talked about my dad, but she did say at least twice that it had been worth it, being that in love.

But how could that be? If I gave up forever with Tom Truby for a few weeks with Nick, and surely that was as long as it would last, would that be worth it? Just to have been his, for him to have been mine, for a short while?

Granted, a few weeks wasn't six years of marriage and two kids. I couldn't see Nick married with children.

"Ruby, your fantasy is telling you he wants you. He's flying here to stop you from marrying another man. You can't get more real than that. You and Nick could very well be the right people for each other, but how could you have ever known before? You've had a boyfriend practically from day one. *You've* made yourself unavailable. And very likely on purpose."

Huh. I hadn't thought of that.

"You, sister dear, are at the fork in the road. One way is the road less traveled by you—the one that doesn't come with a map. The other one is a straight line to Boresville, U.S.A."

She almost had me with her well-used literary reference. But Tom wasn't boring to me. Not at all. He just wasn't Nick. Tom didn't elicit all kinds of adolescent reactions in my body—the racing heart, the sweaty palms, the inability to complete a thought while he looked directly into my eyes.

Okay, so maybe if I were watching Nick up there on the big screen, that face and body magnified, and then the credits rolled and the lights came on and there was Tom Truby sitting next to me with his pleasant face and warm smile and comforting sweater-vest, I would feel that momentary pang, that sigh of *if only*. But that was what fantasy was all about. And wasn't *fantasy* the key word?

9

Close to midnight, Nick arrived on the doorstep of The Double Sisters Inn, a backpack slung over his shoulder. He wore a dark-green T-shirt and jeans and Pumas, and there was five o'clock shadow involved. With his fair skin and those dark, dark eyes and long, dark lashes, he looked like a movie star. As I watched the taxi speed down the dirt road, dust flying, I started to panic.

I will not cheat on Tom. I will not cheat on Tom. I will not cheat on Tom.

I repeated it over and over as I led Nick to my room. To talk. There were two other guest rooms available for him to choose from. The Jesse James room or the Huskers room. Or he could sleep on one of the overstuffed chairs in the parlor. But he was not, under any circumstances, sleeping in my room.

In the small feminine Peaceful room, his presence was too big, the bed looming too large.

"I can't believe you're really here," I said, moving over to the window. I sat down on the chair, and he sat down on the edge of the bed.

"You're halfway to Las Vegas, Ruby. All of a sudden I thought, she's going to arrive in Las Vegas, Truby's going to fly out, and she's going to come back married. And that'll be that. She'll be lost to you."

I did have to credit Nick for not going after married women. The ring on a woman's finger meant something to him; he respected it.

"Nick, I think you're suddenly interested because I'm engaged. And now on a road trip."

"I thought about that," he said, running a hand through his hair. "But I'm not *suddenly* interested, Ruby. I've always been interested. But I've always been…"

"Always been what?"

"Worried about screwing things up. You're my best friend, Ruby. You're the best friend I've ever had. I tell you everything."

I was afraid I'd burst into tears, so I said, "Give me a minute, okay?" and then fled into the bathroom, where I sat on the rim of the clawfoot tub and tried to catch my breath.

Right then, right at that moment, Tom Truby was home in Blueberry Hills, sitting on the sofa with Marco and grading his summer-school essays while every now and then giving Marco a scratch. Maybe he was watching The History Channel or a movie. But he was home, unaware that the woman he lived with, the woman who claimed to love him, the woman he loved, was now in a hotel room with another man, having this conversation. In the immortal words of Joan Armatrading, it made him into "some kind of a unknowing fool." It wasn't fair.

Nick would have to go. End of story.

But then I opened the bathroom door, and he looked up at me, and I knew he wasn't going anywhere.

"Can I stay here with you?" he asked. "I won't touch you, I promise. Unless you want me to. I just want to lie here with you. I want to know what that's like."

We'd laid in bed together before. Many times, many beds, fully clothed. I'd always felt the air whooshing out of my body, while Nick would be recounting his latest drama.

I wanted to kiss him. I now understood how an addict must feel, physically, mentally, and emotionally craving something, like a cigarette, wanting to so bad, yet knowing intellectually it was bad for you. Might kill you, in fact. I wanted to feel his lips on mine, his arms around me in a very unfriendly way. I wanted those dark, dark eyes to be looking into mine with that Nick McDermott intensity.

He stood up, and again the room got too small.

"I won't cheat on Tom," I said. "Not even a kiss, Nick. I won't do that to him. If I want to be with you, if I want to even just kiss you, I need to break up with Tom."

I tried to read his face, tried to remember everything Stella had told me about the pupils dilating—or was it the opposite? But Nick didn't start sweating or pale or visibly tremble at the mention of my breaking up with Tom before I'd even consider a kiss.

That would be heavy, a lot to take on. Let us see if McDreamy was up for it.

He stared at me, then took a deep breath and said, "That's why I want you. Because of who you are."

Shit.

Shit. Shit. Shit.

Now what?

Now you lay down in bed—after brushing your teeth twice and changing into comfortable yet not sexy pajamas—and see if you can actually keep your hands to yourself.

I headed back into the bathroom with my nonclingy sweats and a T-shirt. Washed my face. Brushed my teeth. Twice. I was as fresh scrubbed and unsexy as I could get. Though Tom always told me he found me incredibly sexy like that. I stared at myself in the mirror for a good long time, trying to find some answer in my reflection, in my eyes.

Get out there.

I opened the door and Nick McDermott lay there on the bed, his hands crossed behind his head. The green T-shirt had risen up to reveal his rock-hard stomach. I had the urge to trail kisses across it, slip my hand up under his shirt. Down below the snap of his jeans.

I took a deep breath and lay down next to him. He

turned on his side and looked at me with those eyes. To kiss him, to make out with Nick McDermott, who was mine for the taking, all I had to do was lift my chin and kiss him. Just press my lips to his.

I'd told him I wouldn't cheat on Tom, so I knew he wouldn't make the first move. That was Nick being a gentleman.

I will not cheat on Tom. I will not cheat on Tom. I will not cheat on Tom.

You will not cheat yourself, I heard Stella's voice say in my head. *If you don't find out how you feel, if you don't go for it, whatever it is, you can't possibly make a decision.*

Was I rationalizing my desire to kiss Nick? To sleep with him? Maybe.

He touched the ends of my hair. "Ruby, I want you right now more than anything in the world. But, I'm not going to pressure you. If you need me to find another room, I'll go."

I leaned forward and kissed him, a soft kiss on his lips.

"Is that an invitation?" he asked.

Maybe the sex will be awful, I told myself. We'll have no chemistry. Kissing Nick will feel like kissing the brother I never had. His hands will feel clammy on me. We'll be awkward and knock our heads together. The fantasy and the reality will not meet.

But I knew that wouldn't be the case. Every bit of my body was pulsating. I nodded, then kissed him again. I felt his restraint; he was giving me one more second to change my mind. And then he took over. His hands slid under my tank top, and in seconds we were both naked.

"I've wanted to do this from the moment I saw you," I whispered.

"Me, too," he breathed into my ear, his hands and mouth exploring every inch of me.

And then just like that, the guy of my dreams was doing things to me that I had fantasized about over and over. And the reality was even better.

He was still asleep when I woke up. Sun streamed through the window, lighting the sheer panels against the peach velvet drapes, lighting his dark hair. Nick was on his stomach, facing me, and I was mesmerized by how his eyelashes lay on his cheek. He was so beautiful.

I could still feel the imprint of his lips on mine, on my body. And, yes, the earth had moved. Over and over.

There was a light tap on the door. Stella. I opened the door a crack and she poked her head through.

"Ooh!" she whispered. "Ooh! I am so proud of you!"

"Shush!" I hissed.

She tried to read my face, then burst into a smile. "Guess I should tell Maxine and Charlotte that we'll be staying one more night?"

I shook my head. "He'll have to get back today for school tomorrow. And we need to be in Denver by sundown if we want to stay on track."

"There is no 'on track,' Rubes," she said and blew a kiss at me before disappearing into her room.

I shut the door and tiptoed into the bathroom with my

toiletries and clothes. One quick, hot shower later, and I was ready to face him. I stared at myself in the round mirror over the sink and had to admit I was glowing. I added a little mascara, fluffed my hair a bit more than normally, and put on the pretty cotton little dress that Stella had bought. It was perfect for a hot Sunday morning.

I stared at myself in the mirror to see if I looked different, if I looked like a woman who had cheated on her fiancé, on the man she professed to love and had promised to marry. I didn't look different. I didn't even look guilty. And strangest of all, I didn't *feel* guilty. Because being with Nick was right? Or because being with Nick was the right thing to do under the circumstances? The circumstances being utter and complete confusion.

I am sorry, Tom, I whispered to the air, then closed my eyes and sat down on the rim of the tub. *The earth moves with you a lot, too.*

When I came out of the bathroom, Nick was sitting up and grinning at me.

"You look very pretty," he said. "But I wish you were still naked."

I smiled. "The bright light of day and all…"

"Gotcha. Give me five minutes in the shower and then maybe we could go for a walk or sit somewhere. A cornfield, a coffee bar, whatever."

I nodded and he walked past me into the bathroom with his backpack. I immediately pictured him naked. Felt every part of him on me and in me.

I had to get out of there. I had to breathe, to think. I wrote a quick note for him to meet me in the parlor, then I tiptoed out of the room so that Stella wouldn't hear me and attack me in the hallway. I ducked into the utility closet with a few brooms and breathed in and out.

Why wasn't it clear? Had I chosen Nick by sleeping with him? Is that what it meant? Is that why I'd done it? I closed my eyes and breathed in and out twenty-five times. I heard the sound of a door opening and closing, then footsteps. Nick. I waited a moment, then headed into the parlor.

We had the room to ourselves. Stella had either gone back to sleep or was giving us space. I could hear the Holcomb sisters in the kitchen, preparing for the breakfast hour.

Nick sat across from me at a round table near the window. "I like Tom," he said. "I feel like a jerk for trying to steal his woman away from him. But, Ruby, I'm dead serious. I think I'm in love with you."

Oh, God. If Maxine hadn't come in just then with a basket of minimuffins and a plate of various jams and jellies, I might have fainted. She set down our coffees and our orange juices.

"Well, hello," Maxine said to Nick. "Any friend of Ruby's is a friend of The Double Sisters Inn. What can I get you?"

Nick asked for the house special, whatever that was, and I said make it two. Naturally charmed, Maxine flitted off through the swinging door into the kitchen.

"You think you're in love with me?" I repeated. "Just like that."

"Not just like that. I know I've always had feelings for you, Ruby. But there's something very true-blue about you. I wasn't willing to mess with you."

"Yet you're willing now? When I'm engaged? When you could destroy my future with Tom? When you could decide next week that you're not in love after all?"

"I'm sure I want to try a relationship with you, Ruby. That's what I know for sure. I couldn't just let you go without saying something. Without telling you how I feel. Of course I don't know if it'll work, if we'll work as anything other than best friends. And if it doesn't work, maybe it will destroy the friendship. But how can I not be willing to try?"

If I was truly in love with Nick, wouldn't I be jumping into his arms, telling him I loved him, too, dragging him back to my room to make mad, passionate love all day? Why was I sitting there, holding a container of strawberry jam and feeling so suddenly numb?

Because I was scared? Because what I'd always wanted was being offered to me? A be careful what you wish for?

Or because I loved Tom?

I didn't know through the muffin course, or the eggs and bacon course or the fruit course. Or the second or third cup of coffee. I didn't know when Stella came in, in the white version of my dress, and sat at a different table and asked Maxine if she could whip up chocolate chip scrambled eggs, which sounded revolting.

"Nick, did you know Stella is a sought-after face reader?" I asked him.

He looked confused. "Did you say a face reader?"

"I would love to read your face," Stella said, coming over. She pulled up a chair and stared at him before he could say a word.

He started to get uncomfortable after twenty seconds. Still, she stared, without letting up. "What is it saying?" he asked.

She glanced from him to me and back to him again. "For the first time in my career, I am stumped. I can't read you."

What? The one time I actually could use her mumbo jumbo and she "couldn't read him"?

"Try harder," I told her.

The first time I saw Nick McDermott, he was tutoring a student, a small-for-his-age nervous seventh grader who appeared on the verge of tears. Apparently, the boy had spent forty minutes of class time not writing a word of his essay test, only his name and then three words: *Johnny Tremain was*

"What happened after you wrote *was?*" Nick asked him.

The thin shoulders slumped, then shrugged, then the boy burst into tears.

I stood outside the door, unable to walk away.

Nick got the boy a chair and pulled his own around to sit beside him. "You froze up?" he asked. "Forgot every word of *Johnny Tremain?* Forgot all the good points you wanted to make?"

The boy stopped crying and looked up at Nick and nodded, and I knew right then that Nick was special, that McDreamy aside, he was more than just a good teacher. He was magic.

"I even liked the book," the boy said. "I liked how Johnny was kind of a jerk in the beginning, but then his life got ruined, and he stopped being a jerk." He stared down at his sneakers. "I wish that would happen to some kids I know. Like if a dog bit off Jeff Clarkson's pitching hand, he wouldn't think he ruled BLA anymore."

Nick smiled. "So write that. That's your homework tonight, Jesse. Write *that* essay, about how what happens to Johnny relates to your life, what it makes you think of, and how you feel about it. If you do refer to BLA kids, give them secret code names, like Potatohead. And use at least three examples from the book. Seven hundred fifty words typed. Hand it in tomorrow, and I won't take off any points for not getting it done in class."

The boy brightened. "Really?"

"Really."

The boy walked out, shoulders squared, chin up. That was when Nick noticed me in the hall.

"That was beautiful," I said like an idiot.

Nick smiled at me with that smile, the one that disarmed everyone. "Thanks. Does that mean I can take you to lunch? If you're the new teacher I've heard about."

I wasn't sure if he was asking me out on a date or just being friendly on the new teacher's first day. I was a midterm replacement, and starting in medias res was never easy.

"Actually, my new boss has that covered," I said. "But thank you."

"Another time then," he said, and I could barely look away from those eyes.

As I was leaving Nick's classroom, I ran smack into Tom Truby. He glanced at Nick, then smiled at me.

"I'd better work fast, huh?" Tom said.

"Excuse me?"

"If you've already met McDermott, I'd better ask you out right away."

I laughed. "It's amazing that on my first day here, two men have asked me out. At my last school, not one date."

"They must have all been married," he said. "If you like Indian food, there's a very good place in Portland. In the Old Port." He was looking at me the way Nick had been looking at me. But Tom was looking at me seriously, earnestly, whereas there had been a sparkle in Nick's eyes. The love of the game, the hunt, the flirt.

I had dinner with Tom that very night. Over chicken tikka and Taj Mahal beer, I discovered that true as his name, Tom Truby was also funny, chivalrous, charming, kind, smart, all good things. Granted, he didn't have the same physical effect on me that Nick did. But by the next time Nick asked me out for lunch, Tom and I were already a couple, so Nick and I drifted into a friendship that I never expected would become so close, so necessary.

Stella's face reading made Nick so uncomfortable that he got up and said he'd like to walk around the property, see a bit of Nebraska before he'd have to head back. The farmhouse sat on three acres, and from the back porch that wrapped around the house, you could stare out onto gently rolling hills and have a good think.

Nick and I sat on the chaise longues, two glasses of iced teas on the table between us.

"You don't think I'm serious, do you?" he said. "You think once I win you away from Truby, I'll lose interest."

"Part of me is worried about that, Nick. But that's not really the question here."

"What is the question?" he asked.

"The question is—how do I really, really feel?"

"How *do* you feel?"

"All I know for sure is that I *should* know. In order to make a decision, I mean. About being with you. About marrying Tom. I should know how I feel. And I don't. How scary is that?"

"You don't have to know, Ruby. You don't always have to know how you feel. Sometimes you have to find your way to the answer. I guess that's what you're doing now. Why you said yes last night." He smiled at me and reached for my hand. "We were pretty amazing."

I smiled back. "We were."

We stood up, and he kissed me, a long, delicious kiss that was every bit heartfelt as it was passionate. Then he pulled back and looked at me, squeezed my hand, and was gone.

10

I USED THE I-DON'T-WANT-TO-TALK-ABOUT-IT RESPONSE THAT
Stella had taught me, and she got so fed up she finally went
into her room to pack. There was nothing to tell her,
nothing to say. "I don't know" was actually the only answer
that came to me.

I went into the parlor for a cup of tea and with a novel
I'd been meaning to find time to start. But I couldn't concentrate and ended up reading the first paragraph four times.

I closed the book and stared out the window, trying not
to think about men.

Scratch that. I decided to dedicate my brain to another
man: figuring out a plan for finding Jake or Jason or James
in Las Vegas. His name would probably turn out to be
Stephen.

"Did your friend leave?" Maxine asked, coming in to refill the sugar bowls.

I nodded. "Maxine, how did you know that Nick was just a friend and not my fiancé?"

"I suppose you didn't seem like a couple."

I stared at her. "How could you tell?" Aside from V Squared, most couples didn't get all PDA in restaurants, did they?

"Let me ask you before I put my foot in my mouth," she said. "Was that your fiancé? Did I get it wrong?"

"No."

She smiled. "Well, despite what Stella said, about you not loving your fiancé, or not being sure, I sensed something else in you."

I almost started to cry. This conversation reminded me so much of the talks I used to have with my mother, over things big and small. But now I was on my own.

"What did you sense?" I asked.

"Just questions, I suppose," she said. "And I think the best place to find your answers is on the road, like you gals are doing. I always did my best thinking on miles-long walks on the plains. You just need air and time and answers usually present themselves."

I hoped she was right. Because we'd come halfway, and I was no closer.

"Thank you, Maxine," I said, going over to give her a hug. "You're very wise."

She beamed and excused herself to the kitchen.

My cell beeped. Text message from Tom.

EV OK?

I typed back: *Y. XO. R.*

But everything wasn't okay.

We were halfway to Denver when Stella said, "I am so sick of hearing 'I don't know!' Stop saying 'I don't know.'"

I laughed, signaling my intent to move into the fast lane to get around a slowpoke elderly man going ten miles under the speed limit. "Now you know what it feels like."

She took a bite of her McDonald's hamburger, then checked to see if she got her extra pickles and extra ketchup. Seemingly satisfied, she put the bun back on top and took another bite. "He told you he thinks he's in love with you, and you're still questioning?"

"*Thinks* is not *knows,* Stella."

She groaned.

"I *know* I love Tom," I said. "That's never been in doubt."

"Ugh, if you say so. But do you love him enough to spend the rest of your life wondering if you should have given Nick a chance?"

That was the Magic 8 Ball question. Which right now said: *I Don't Know.* And *Ask Again Later.*

Stella popped a malt ball into her mouth. "Every time I used to ask Mom about Dad and how she felt about him, she'd always say she had no regrets. Isn't that crazy?"

"Maybe it's different when you have children," I said. "I

mean, we come along with that regret. If there'd been no Eric Miller in her life, there'd be no us."

"Do you think she would have married him if she'd had that list of questions from the *New York Times* article?"

I shrugged. "I'm sure she had her own checklist. And I'm sure he seemed like a good match, that he'd make her happy, that she'd make him happy."

"Or maybe she didn't ask herself any questions. Maybe she just went with how she *felt*," Stella said.

"Well, if that was the case, it's not like it worked out. Not asking questions. Maybe if she'd asked some important questions about compatibility, she would have realized he wasn't the right person for her." I shook my head. "Or maybe he just changed. I don't know. It just seems to me that you know, from somewhere deep inside you, what's right for you, and you either listen to it or not."

"And you know deep inside that Tom is the right person?" she asked. "Even after sleeping with Nick, you still know for sure?"

I burst into tears. "I don't know anything."

"Rubes," she said, rubbing my back. "You'll figure it out. I'll shut up, okay?"

"Promise?" I asked.

She laughed. "Promise."

Four hours later, we arrived at our hotel in Denver, the majestic peaks of the Rockies visible from our room. I was dying to get out and explore, to forget everything crowding my head and just appreciate the gorgeous vistas, but lying down for a half hour turned into all night. When we woke up, the sun streamed through the windows right into my face. Stella wasn't feeling so hot and just wanted to get in the car and go. The plan was to drive four hours to Grand Junction, stop for the night, and from there drive to Richfield, Utah. And then finally, we would take off for the final leg of our road trip.

We ended up spending two nights in Grand Junction because Stella's "I'm not feeling so hot" turned out to be a bad cold that knocked her out the first day. Grand Junction was Colorado's wine country, and we'd planned on a tour or two, but it was over ninety-five degrees and Stella wasn't up for anything but bed and a cold compress and her *Girlfriends' Guide To Pregnancy*. She got all guilty about making me miss out on some of the most beautiful parts of the United States, but I reminded her that this trip wasn't so much about sightseeing as it was getting to where we were going.

I did some serious walking in Grand Junction, hoping the open air would whisper some truths in my ear, about what I wanted, how I felt. But there was just more of nothing, a blank line where a name might go. The walk that was supposed to calm me down got me so riled that I picked up a rock and threw it as far as I could, aiming for a wooden sign on the side of the road about fifty feet in front of me. Bull's-eye. There was something satisfying about hitting my mark.

"Could you please not throw rocks at my sign?"

I whirled around, and there, on an ancient yellow bike

with a basket, was a tall, very tanned, almost leathery woman, her long, brown hair in a braid down her back. She wore a beige leotard, and because her skin was pretty much the same color, I thought she was naked at first.

"If something's bothering you enough to throw a rock, you might want to meditate," she said, getting off the bike and setting the kickstand. "You're welcome to use my studio." She gestured behind her. "My class won't start for another couple of hours."

I glanced behind her. On this stretch of rural road, just a mile from the hotel, was absolutely nothing but grass, brownish grass, at that, trees, and the majestic mountains in the distance. "Your studio?" I repeated.

"Look more closely," she said.

I walked over to her, and there on the grass were ten straw mats placed rather haphazardly. I looked up at her. "Do you mean these?"

She nodded. "Choose one and lie down and close your eyes. Silently say the word *peace* seven times. Then think about peace."

"Right now?"

She smiled and stepped aside. I wondered if she had a portable CD player and if Enya would blare at me at any moment. I chose a mat right in the middle of the ten.

"Interesting choice," she said. "You feel bombarded."

Oh, c'mon. I squinted up at her. "Wouldn't I have chosen a mat on the edges, then? For breathing room? Or to run away easier?"

"We tend to choose the comfortable, the familiar, over and over. If you'd chosen a mat on the edge, I would be less concerned for your spirit. Now, close your eyes."

I let out a deep breath and closed my eyes, then sat up and turned around. "For how long?" I asked her.

"As long as it takes," she said and sat down across the road in some kind of yoga position, her palms up on her thighs.

I lay back down, closed my eyes and said *peace* to myself seven times. By number four, I started thinking about my mother, her round hazel eyes, their flutter of lashes. That her favorite color was turquoise. That every night she would open to the dinner section of *Have Fun Cooking With Kids* and randomly pick a page. Then the three of us—Mom and Stella and I—would go to the supermarket with the recipe, and come back home and cook together.

Which made me think of the last time Tom and I cooked together, the night we got engaged. Yes, he'd proposed on the stairs. During fourth period. But he'd also had my mother's ring in a beautiful velvet-lined box that he presented to me and then slid on my finger when I said yes.

That night, Tom had taken me to dinner at my favorite restaurant and arranged for three opera singers to sing with their "inside voices" (I loved opera). We'd been too full for dessert, so we'd gone home, planning to open another bottle of champagne, but while I was getting the corkscrew, Tom Truby very uncharacteristically began undressing me in the kitchen. We'd made love right on the kitchen floor, in front of the little island. And then we'd gotten to work, measuring flour and cracking eggs and melting bittersweet chocolate for a tiny chocolate cake for two. We ate our cake on the porch swing, our special place, just before midnight.

At peace number seven, Nick's face floated into my mind. Cooking seemed to be the theme of peace for some reason. We were at his apartment on a Saturday morning, creating a curriculum for an elective course in multicultural poetry. All of a sudden it was lunchtime and we were starving, so I explored his refrigerator and cupboards and put together a picnic lunch that we took out to the promenade. A seagull had been patiently waiting for a crumb or two, and Nick made the mistake of being generous and then we were surrounded by the birds, hoping and waiting. I took a great photograph of him standing up on the bench, half a sandwich in his hands and beaks at the ready.

And then it was Stella, at fifteen, with bright-pink hair that took forever to color over. And Stella and Silas and I at the Blueberry Hills Festival, throwing blueberries at each other's mouths and missing.

My eyes fluttered opened. I stared up at the bright-blue sky with its cotton ball clouds, content to lie there for hours. But then I remembered that I was lying basically on the side of the road, albeit on a wide grassy expanse. I sat up and turned and looked for the tanned woman, but she and her bike were gone.

There was something taped to the wooden sign. I jogged over. It was a note.

Peace seeker with the pretty blond hair: the mat is yours to keep. Use it when you want to throw rocks. —Anne

At that moment, I wanted the three-foot-long straw mat more than I wanted anything. I rolled it up and put it under my arm, then ran back for the note and folded it and put it in my pocket. I ripped off the bottom half and wrote "Thank you so much—Ruby" and used what I could salvage of the tape of her note to tack my note up where hers had been.

By the time I returned to the hotel, I wondered if I'd imagined the entire experience, if it had happened at all, if I'd lain on a yoga mat on the side of a road and thought about peace, about cooking, about the people I loved.

"Hey, what do you have there?" Stella asked, eyeing my mat. "Did you take a yoga class or something?" She sat up a bit, barely able to lift her head. "You look great. So relaxed. You're almost glowing."

I wrote myself a mental note: meditate more often.

The vivid blue sign welcoming us to Utah was the only color in sight as far as the eye could see. Except for Stella's face, which was back to its rosy glow from the depth of bad-cold-itis. She was almost one hundred percent better by the time we saw our first Joshua tree. It had been three days since her throat could handle a malt ball, so she was thrilled to crunch them along I-70, a desolate stretch of highway that still managed to be utterly beautiful with its rocky cliffs and barren hills, the mountains appearing like distant jutting clouds along the landscape.

I'd bought a guidebook that included Utah and Las Vegas and Arizona, which we would only pass through for five minutes before we hit Nevada, and while Stella drove, I did some reading to find out what might be worth stopping to see. Apparently, the entire state was worth stopping to see, but Stella thought we lost too much time in Colorado.

As Mainers, Stella and I knew from breathtaking scenery, but at one point, we were in such awe of the landscape that Stella pulled over and we got out just to stare, just to see absolutely nothing but land and mountains for miles in any direction. According to the guidebook, the best was yet to come, in Southern Utah, where we'd descend from the mountain region into the high desert with its red rock and buttes and mesas. Where we'd drive through the Virgin River Gorge, created from cliffs that jutted out on both sides of the freeway. You could forget about cell phone reception until you exited. And when you did you'd be in Nevada.

"This totally makes me understand why people get so outdoorsy and go hiking and climb mountains," Stella said, taking a photo of nothing but brown expanse.

Or meditate on straw mats on the side of the road, with the birds and quiet wind for music.

Despite being Mainers, we were New York City kids at heart, and our hearts seemed to be in observing people rather than land. We were both shoppers, eavesdroppers on conversations, and liked our lattes. But this trip instilled a new appreciation for nature in both of us, in just breathing pure clean air.

We stopped for the night in a town called Beaver City. Our hotel appeared to be built out of rock. The super chatty desk clerk, a forty-something man with the bluest eyes I'd ever seen, told us that Beaver City was the birthplace of Butch Cassidy and Philo T. Farnsworth, inventor of the television. I had him write that down on the motel stationery for Tom. I knew he'd like that.

The clerk recommended a bunch of places for us to visit, including the inactive volcanoes and the Wal-Mart in Colorado City, the polygamist enclave, where we could see women with sister wives and cartfuls of well-behaved children up close. Stella's eyes lit up at the thought of interviewing a diner waitress who shared her husband with many women, but then decided we should stick to the plan of leaving first thing in the morning and not stopping until we hit Sin City. That still didn't stop us from staying up past midnight, laughing about how the same man would never go for both Stella and me, that we were way too different, just like Maxine and Charlotte. But then Stella reminded me that Danny Peel, back in kindergarten, couldn't choose between us and said he wanted us both to be his girlfriend, because, and I quote: "I have two hands, don't I?" He slipped one into mine and one into Stella's and off we'd gone to the playground. The trio actually lasted the entire school year.

11

TWO MINUTES ON THE LAS VEGAS STRIP, AND WE ALMOST collided with a white limo, a drunk bride's head poking out of the sun roof.

"I *did!*" the bride trilled, then took a swig out of a bottle of wine. "I *did!* Whoo-*hoooooo!*" I shot her a thumbs-up and she let out the loudest scream of joy I'd ever heard.

It was an appropriate welcome to Sin City, which looked exactly like I imagined. Times Square had nothing on Vegas. Humongous hotels of different glowing colors, from pink to green. Hundreds, thousands maybe, of people walked up and down the boulevard, and the cars, adding to the glow of color with their red taillights, were a steady, slow-moving stream.

Stella had booked us into the New York-New York Hotel & Casino on Las Vegas Boulevard; she felt that because her child had been conceived in New York, New York, it was the place to start three thousand miles away. It was as good a starting place as any other—an ice cream parlor, a dentist's office, a blackjack table. Or the four thousand-plus hits on Google for *law office, Las Vegas.*

We stood outside the massive-never-seen-anything-like-it hotel, staring up and around and over and down. The New York-New York was such an incredible feat of architecture meets facade meets *wow* meets theme park, that I wasn't even bothered by the one-hundred-seven-degree temperature. There was a one-hundred-fifty-foot Statue of Liberty and a stunning replica of the Empire State Building. Inside, a real live roller coaster looped around the hotel. Good thing Stella was pregnant, or she might have tried to talk me into it.

We were paying a fortune for the stay. It was a good thing we were sinking our money into the hotel; we would not be tempted to do *anything* (code word for "waste money on slot machines") other than look for J.

Our room, which took some doing to find, had two queen-size beds with cacti on the headboards, which was the only reminder that we were in Las Vegas and not New York. We both took showers, then got ready for dinner (and, yes, we were definitely planning on using our two-for-one coupon for the fancy New York-style steak house).

"Let's dress up," Stella said. "I'm feeling lucky."

"What does that mean?"

"It means I feel really hopeful. Like I might really find him, Ruby."

I stared at my sister, fresh out of the shower, her hair plastered wet against her shoulders. For the first time I understood, really understood, what my mother had meant about the just-rolled-out-of-bed-to-breakfast look. Here Stella was, no artifice, no tiny tank top with some aggressive saying or message across her ample chest, no yoga pants that showed her abs and belly button. No shimmery lip gloss or Paris Hilton-esque sunglasses. She was just Stella. A pregnant Stella looking for the father of her baby.

"I feel lucky, too," I told her, squeezing her hand. "Are you going to wear the dress you bought at the Kittery outlets?"

She nodded and took it out of her suitcase. It looked great. That was the thing about slinky jersey—it never wrinkled. The dress was sleeveless red and halter style. "Red is my color according to Maxine. I miss her," she said, sitting down on the edge of her bed, the dress folded on her lap. "Didn't she and Charlotte sort of remind you of Mom?"

I'd had the same thought back at The Double Sisters Inn. Nebraska seemed so long ago, Nick's visit like a dream. "I forgot how much I missed talking to her, telling her things. I could ask her what she thinks of all this with Tom and Nick."

"Would you have told her?" Stella asked.

"Probably not," I said. "She'd have gotten it out of me, though. She would have known something was wrong."

"I knew something was wrong," she said, glancing up at me.

"I know. I guess you know me better than I thought."

"But you're still not going to tell me what you're going to do?" she asked. "Are you going to marry Nick instead?"

I raised an eyebrow. "I think you're forgetting that Nick hasn't proposed anything other than a chance. He wants to date me."

"And you…"

"And I wish things could stay the same. I could be engaged to Tom, like permanently, and have my secret fantasy crush on Nick, neither moving ahead."

She nodded. "I feel that way about this sometimes," she said, patting her belly. "If I could just freeze time until I found J…"

"Guess time and life move on whether we're ready or not," I said, glancing out the window at the lights and whir of constant movement.

She smiled and disappeared into the bathroom with her dress and cosmetics bag. I pawed through my own suitcase for the one nice dress I'd packed, a pale-yellow silk wrap dress, and my high-heeled silver sandals.

The last time we got ready like this was for the senior prom. Silas was her date, and we all expected him to come to the house in some crazy outfit to protest the ordinary and expected, but he showed up in a classic tuxedo. Stella was sure he'd done it for our mother, who'd talked about nothing but the prom to us for weeks prior. She must have checked the batteries in her camera a thousand times. Stella told her she probably wouldn't want keepsake memories of

Silas in a T-shirt and jeans and Doc Martens at the BLA senior prom, but my mother said she most certainly would. And then Silas arrived in the tux.

My date was my boyfriend at the time, a nice guy named Nathanial, but he and Silas did not speak the same language and so the four of us barely saw each other at the prom. I'd forgotten about Nathanial, how Stella yawned behind his back and told me I could do "so much better." I'd thought she was being a bratty snob and it made me want to fall in love with Nathanial all the more. While I was trying hard, he found love with some girl he was working with at a dairy farm. *Not every hot guy will be like Mark Feeler,* she would say. *You don't have to date these bores. Let me tell you, a bore will break your heart and dump you same as a hot guy. Emily Patcher just got dumped by her dweebinski boyfriend, and she's totally brokenhearted!*

I'd thought about that lately. Wondered if I'd said yes to certain guys over the years because of the Mark Feeler debacle. Because of the Eric Miller disappearance. If you weren't in love, you couldn't get your heart blown to bits. I supposed that might apply to my current love life. I wasn't quite "in love" with Tom, my fiancé, and I was madly in love with Nick, my fantasy crush. Who I hadn't said yes to.

"Ruby!" Stella said as she came out of the bathroom. "You look hot!"

I laughed. "It's my one fancy dress."

"You should wear it every night," she said, linked arms with me, and off we went.

★ ★ ★

As we waited for our Perriers in the steak house, I got down to business, a small spiral notebook open and pen at the ready. I wanted every detail of the night Stella and J met. The name of the bar, what they drank, how they hooked up in the first place, what he said, what she said, where they went afterward—before her apartment.

"I told you everything, Ruby."

"No, you told me some basics. I want every detail. If you want to find this guy, tell me everything."

"Okay, here's everything. I was waiting at the bar inside Georgina's, an Italian restaurant on Columbus. Corner of Seventy-fourth," Stella said as the waiter delivered our drinks. "I was supposed to meet a potential client—a new painter who was blocked—but he never showed up. So twenty minutes later, I was getting up to leave, and the man who'd been a few seats down said, 'You were stood up, too?' So I asked if he was the painter, Pierre Something, and he said, no, his name was Jake. Or something like it." She sipped her water. "You know, Ruby, I think it was Jake. Not James or Jason."

"Okay, I'm going to stop you right there. Just concentrate on him at the bar, telling you his name. What does he look like? What's he wearing?"

She closed her eyes. "A suit. I'd forgotten that! A nice suit. All I remembered before was that he wore a nice button-down dress shirt and nice dark pants. Oh, and he had a brief-case with his—" She stopped, her mouth dropping open.

"What? Monogram? His initials? Stella, that's great! Do you think you can remember the initials? Close your eyes and—"

"Ruby, I think that's him," she said, her gaze trailing a man who followed a hostess to a table across the restaurant. "I think that's him!"

I stared from him to Stella. "Really? Are you sure?"

He was sitting a good distance away; two tables blocked our view. From this vantage point, I could only see that he was tall, attractive, dark-haired, and bore a striking resemblance to Hugh Jackman.

She squinted in his direction. "I think so! He looks exactly like him."

Talk about odds. There were clearly karmic influences at work. Forces of the universe.

She bit her lip. "Now that I actually found him without meaning to, I don't know what to do. What do I say? Do I say anything?" She held the menu up to her face, peeking out every two seconds.

"Go over there and start with hello," I said.

"Okay, sure. I'll just say, 'Hello, um, you might not remember me, but three months ago, we had a one-night stand, not that it wasn't memorable, because it was, and it turns out that I'm pregnant. Congratulations! You're going to be a father.'"

"You might leave out the last two bits, Stella, but that first really long run-on sentence will do just fine."

"Really?" she asked. "I should just say that? Just spit it out?"

We spent the next five minutes working on her great

speech. She would go over to his table and say, "Hi, I think we met in New York three months ago," with something of a question mark, and then he would burst up out of his seat and say, "Stella, is it really you? I've been looking all over the continent for you!"

"I can fantasize," she said. "Okay, I'm ready." She stood up and smoothed her dress and took three quick deep breaths.

She'd barely put one foot in front of the other when a very attractive redhead in a low-cut glittering silver gown was led to his table. He stood, she sat, he sat, and the killer kiss put V Squared's best PDA to shame. The man's hand was practically inside her décolletage.

"Oh," Stella said, her face crumpling as she dropped back on her chair.

Oh no was more like it.

"Stella, remember, he doesn't know about the baby. He just knows that he had an amazing connection with a woman on a one-night stand and then wasn't able to find her again. And I'm sure he looked. I'm sure he went back to that restaurant and the other places you went afterward. I'm sure he walked all around your neighborhood, trying to remember which building could possibly be yours. Once he finds you again, I'm sure the redhead will be history. They probably met five minutes ago in the casino."

"Do you really think so?" she asked, brightening. "Only couples who met five minutes ago would be all over each other like that, right?"

"Definitely," I said.

The couple sitting at the table closer to ours got up and left, so now there was only one couple blocking our view of J and the redhead. They could easily see us, too, and it seemed that he glanced over a time or two, as if checking out the two hot babes in the sexy dresses.

If he recognized Stella, he didn't show it.

"He doesn't even remember me!" she whispered. "He just looked right at me. Not a flicker of recognition."

"Well, you probably weren't wearing a sexy cocktail dress with your hair in a glamorous updo when you met," I reminded her.

"Actually, I was. I was on a muse interview, remember? Muses don't wear jeans and fleece sweaters."

I would think that plenty of more "natural" women inspired artists—Grand Junction Anna, with her yellow bike and roadside meditation classes, was probably an unintentional muse to many—but now wasn't the time to debate the qualities of a muse.

"I'm a professional," she added, as though she read my mind.

The waiter came over, but we asked for a few minutes to decide on the menu. Not that either of us could eat a bite.

J and the redhead were now sipping champagne, their arms linked. The routine went like this: sip, kiss, sip, kiss, sip, kiss.

"Okay, I have a plan," I said, shoving my Perrier out of hand-talking zone. "I think you should just go over there and say the same thing we'd already worked out. In slightly less romantic-sounding terms."

"Example?"

"I think you should pretend you're on your way to the restroom, then stop dead in your tracks and say, 'Excuse me, but you look *so* familiar. I could swear we met in New York City a few months ago.'"

"That sounds pretty good," she said. "Very natural." She closed her eyes and let out a deep breath. "I'm so nervous," she added. "But here goes." She stood up, then sat down.

I squeezed her hand. "If he says, 'you must be mistaken,' and runs out, then, okay, that's the worst-case scenario, and I'll be right here. But there he is, the holder of the other chromosome. The father of your baby," I whispered. "Go."

She gnawed, sipped her water, peered at herself in her compact, took another deep breath, did all of that all over again, and then stood. "Okay." Then she sat back down. "Can I just write it on a napkin and airplane it over?"

I squeezed her hand. "Cloth napkins don't airplane over. Be brave, Stell."

"Okay," she said again. "Here goes everything."

I smiled and nodded. As she stood up, I realized she was about to change a person's entire life in a moment. Of course, she'd already had that moment herself in a bathroom, alone, with a plus sign on a pregnancy test. And she did fine. No matter what Jake or James or Jason had to say, she would be fine.

She sat back down. "I need a minute, Ruby."

"You don't have a minute," I said. "They're leaving!"

J threw a bill on the table. Then, with their arms around each other, they kissed their way out of the restaurant, the redhead walking remarkably steady in four-inch heels.

"We can't let him just walk out, never to be seen again," Stella said. "We have to follow him."

Feeling very Hollywood, I threw some bills on the table and Stella and I hurried after them. But between the crowds and the waiters carrying huge round trays piled with fifty-dollar steaks and twenty-five-dollar drinks, we were too slow to get to the door and the couple was gone.

12

STELLA WAS ON THE VERGE OF TEARS. "I CAN'T BELIEVE IT. WHY did I hesitate? How could I have let him get away?"

I glanced all over the hallways and lobby, and thanks to Jake or Jason or James's date's glittering gown, I spotted first her, then him, among a crowd by the elevator bank.

"Ruby, there they are!" I said, gesturing. I felt like shouting "After them!"

We raced over on our own high heels. Because this was Las Vegas, no one paid the slightest attention to us. We got to the elevator bank just as J and his date disappeared into one of the twenty or so elevators. Stella stuck her clutch purse in the door, and it opened slightly, but then shut again. Stella pulled it out, and a few beads fell to the carpet.

"They were in there alone," I said. "Let's just watch to see what floor it stops on."

Please don't stop at a bunch of floors, I prayed. If it did, it would mean people were getting on and off and we would have no idea where J was going.

The elevator was an express. It stopped at the sixteenth floor. And then started coming back down! Which meant the father of my niece or nephew was somewhere on the sixteenth floor.

An elevator pinged open and we rushed in and hit Sixteen and then Door Closed just as another couple was about to step in. I shouted a "Sorry!" and willed the elevator to go faster.

The elevator door opened on the sixteenth floor. There was a long hallway, hundreds of closed doors. To the right was a nook with a huge ficus tree and a window, the glittering lights of Vegas stunning at this height.

And behind that huge ficus tree was a couple having sex. I heard the moans first, then saw the flashes of movement. J and the redhead were going at it. He was behind her, her dress up around her hips. Both their hands were braced against the wall. Given their inability to wait until after their meal had been served, it was no surprise that they'd been unable to wait to get inside their room.

In the space of about two weeks, this was the second time I'd witnessed a couple having sex in a public place.

"Oh, God," Stella whispered, her hand flying to her mouth. "I'm going to be sick."

"I'm really sorry," I whispered back.

We could hear him moaning. We could hear her breathily saying, "But someone could see us," over and over again with feigned concern. Clearly they enjoyed the possibility.

Was I supposed to discreetly cough? Was Stella supposed to say—while he was in midthrust—*Oh, excuse me, didn't we meet in New York three months ago? Remember when it was us going at it all night long?*

Stella backed into the slight enclave of a doorway. "I guess we have to wait till they're done, then pretend we just came out of the room."

"Oh, oh-oh," the redhead woman moaned. "Someone might see us. Ohh."

Stella was close to tears. I was tapping my fingers against my hips. You'd think they wouldn't be so *leisurely* in a public hallway. Stella stared at her feet. "This is the father of Silas or Clarissa?" she whispered to me. "How could I have been so stupid?"

"Don't beat yourself up," I whispered back.

I heard a giggle, then a woman's voice say, "What a lovely view of the strip!"

I glanced over. Glitzy and J were now looking out the window. He appeared to be adjusting his shirt back into his pants, and she was fluffing her hair.

"Okay, Stella, now or never. Let's just act like we're coming down the hall, then you stop and do a double take and tell him he looks so familiar."

We headed down the hall; they came straight at us, their faces flushed, their hair mussed. As we were about to pass, Stella stopped and stared. I saw her almost lose it, but she immediately regained her composure. "Excuse me," she said to J, attempting to smile. "You look so familiar. I think we might have met in New York. Maybe a few months ago? Yes—three months ago on the Upper West Side?"

He smiled. "Sorry, but I haven't visited New York in a couple of years."

She stared at him. "The resemblance is just uncanny," she said, and I could see she was struggling not to fall completely apart. "Georgina's restaurant? I'm so sure it was you!"

"Wait, three months ago?" the redhead said. "We weren't back from Greece yet, were we, baby? We rent a villa in Ios for a few months every spring."

"Hmm, Ios," the man said, and started trailing kisses up the woman's neck. Then they kissed their way down the hall and into a room, the door clicking shut behind them.

"J had brown eyes!" Stella said, grabbing me by the arms. "He had brown eyes! I remember that now. 'Brown Eyed Girl' came on the jukebox at the Irish pub we'd stopped in, and I'd started singing, 'my brown-eyed man' and trying to get him to dance! That guy—" she pointed at the door the couple had disappeared through "—had blue eyes! It wasn't him!" She slid down against the wall onto her butt. She took a deep breath. "Thank God it wasn't him."

If I weren't so relieved, either, I might have tried to strangle her.

★ ★ ★

We slept late. For such a loud city that operated twenty-four hours a day, our room was so quiet—and we were clearly so drained—that we didn't open our eyes until after nine. Hot showers woke us both up, as did a quick cup of the in-room coffee, which Stella made while I was brushing my teeth.

"I'm not going to find him," she said, pulling on her jeans. "I know it."

"You might." I'd say the chances were close to zero, given that she didn't even know what he looked like. She had an idea only at this point. But his actual face had faded from her memory.

She put on a white tank top with ruffles down the front. "Why'd you even say yes to this trip? You knew we wouldn't find him, that it was a ridiculous prospect. So why'd you say yes? Why were you willing to drive three thousand miles?"

"To support you," I said. "That's what sisters do."

She nodded, then disappeared into the bathroom again. When she finally emerged, she looked a bit happier, but it might have been the makeup. "If he lives here, he's probably at work. Maybe we could do an Internet search of all lawyers in Las Vegas named Jake."

"And James and Jason," I said.

"It's a start."

It was. And so we skipped our two-for-one breakfast in the New York–New York Hotel, and went to a coffee lounge with computer kiosks and Internet access.

I typed *lawyer, Jake,* and *Las Vegas* into Google's search engine. Two hundred and sixty-three thousand hits came up for my researching pleasure. "We could type in *Las Vegas* and *lawyer* and try to cull a list of Jakes from all the Las Vegas attorneys," I suggested to Stella, who looked utterly dejected.

"Think we'll find him that way?" she asked.

"No." Especially because she wouldn't even be able to pick him out of a lineup. "But maybe," I said when her face crumpled.

"Sorry, Silas or Clarissa," she whispered in the direction of her belly. Then she got up and hurried out of the café.

I slurped the rest of my coffee, logged out, and chased after her, but she was lost in the crowds of the strip. She could probably use some time and space to herself. And so could I.

I headed back to the hotel, stopping to gawk up at the facades of New York City institutions and landmarks as though I was seeing them for the first time, and then went to the room to get my meditation mat. I didn't know where one could find an expanse of grassy roadside right here in Sin City, but I'd bet they existed.

The little red message light was blinking on the telephone in our room. But it wasn't Stella. It was Tom. And he was here. In the lobby, under a huge lithograph of the Chrysler Building. He'd left the message a half hour ago. Said he'd wait a half hour, then go explore for an hour and come back and try me again.

Tom was here? As in he was expecting to get married tonight? My heart started booming in my chest and I sat down on the edge of my bed. Blank. Nothing. Nick had once told me that when faced with a tough decision, the only way was to pretend that someone was holding a gun to your head and giving you one second to decide. To pick.

I tried to imagine a gun to my head, but the problem was that I couldn't imagine who could possibly be holding the gun, so the urgency I was hoping for didn't materialize. Guess it was a water gun.

I took the meditation mat out of the closet, unrolled it in front of the bed, and lay down. I envisioned Anne on her yellow bike telling me to close my eyes and say the word *peace* seven times. I did what she said, but I couldn't even get to peace number two. Instead, there were miniature men on each of my shoulders, a Tom and a Nick. Miniature Tom wore his Dockers and a sweater-vest, a maroon one. Miniature Nick wore a black shirt and pants. Both their heads were bobbing like mad. The Tom said, *Marry me! I represent the Nathanials! The good guys of the world. The ones who won't break your heart and run away. I have an IRA!* The Nick said, *Don't you want to know what it's like to be with me?*

I opened my eyes. I needed Stella. Not that she would be any help. She would say to choose Nick just because he wasn't Tom. Just then, the miniature Tom punched the miniature Nick off my left shoulder.

Did that mean I wanted Tom to win? Or that he had won? Was the meditation mat supposed to be starting fights?

13

I WAS STILL ON THE MAT WHEN THE PHONE RANG. I JUMPED UP TO answer it, which had to be a sign. "Tom?"

"I hope this is a good surprise," he said.

"Of course it is," I told him. "Room 1622."

I stood in front of the mirror over the bureau to make sure I looked okay, which had to be another good sign. And a few minutes later, there was a knock at the door, and there he was, standing in the doorway. My Tom. My Tom in his Dockers, and his sweater-vest (navy-blue) and his clean, shiny blond hair. And those true-blue blue eyes.

I jumped into his arms and he hugged me tight, carrying me over to the bed, where he lay down on top of me and kissed me. "I have missed you so much," he said, burying his face in my neck.

I kissed him back, breathing in the smell of Ivory soap. "Me, too," I said. "I have a lot to tell you."

"Does it include not wanting to marry me?" he asked.

I don't know. I'm supposed to know, but I don't.

"Why do you think that?" I asked, hating myself for it. That was what manipulators did. Made the other person doubt himself, made the other person even more vulnerable. Only so you could lie right in their face.

He tucked a strand of errant blond hair behind my ear. "I thought you wanted to elope, but when you ignored my text about it, I knew something was up. You worried me, Ruby."

"I didn't mean to." For a moment I thought about telling him everything. Tom was so smart, so insightful, and if I could just tell him everything, all about my first day at BLA, about how I wanted to say yes to Nick but didn't, perhaps he could advise me on whether I owed it to all three of us to give Nick a chance.

Right. Sure, I could tell Tom that. But the story did get better—for him. I had chosen him at every step. Not Nick. Until Nebraska. And now I had a choice to make.

I would not tell Tom all of this. Instead, I would give myself more time, not that this entire trip had brought me one step closer to that answer.

"I'm just so distracted by Stella and her situation," I said, running my hands through his silky hair. I filled him in on everything we'd been through regarding the hunt for the elusive Jake or James or Jason.

"You two tried," he said. "She'll always have that. She'll always know she went to great lengths to try to find him. And how her twin sister was right there with her."

I nodded, and he wrapped his arms around me. We sat like that for a moment. "You know, I flew out here sure that I'd be returning a married man. I figured we'd get married in some ridiculous chapel with a Captain Kirk impersonator presiding. But given what's going on with Stella, we probably shouldn't be marrying in her face."

I hugged him. "That's what I love so much about you, Tom. That you did come out here because you were worried about me. That you were willing to have some stranger in Spock ears officiate at our wedding. And that you care more about Stella's feelings than anything."

He cupped my chin in his hands. "I would do anything for you, Ruby."

I believed he would. "You know, Tom? Now that I've been here a couple of days, I wouldn't want to get married here after all. I thought eloping to Vegas would be special because my parents did that. But we're not them."

He squeezed my hand, then kissed me long and hard. "Meet me in my room in five minutes," he said. "I'll call you with the number."

I put away the meditation mat. Being with Tom was suddenly as good as counting seven peaces.

Stella wasn't answering her cell phone. Stubborn. I'd left a note for her in our room, explaining that Tom had surprised me with a visit and we were in Room 812, but I still hadn't heard from her. Where was she? Out walking the strip? Sitting alone in some coffee lounge drinking decaf and reading *The Girlfriends' Guide to Pregnancy*? Searching high and low for J?

If I knew Stella, and I did, she was sitting by one of the ornate fountains we'd seen yesterday, like the one outside Spago. Stella loved fountains. She'd often told me that when she had a tough decision—or a wish—to make, she would walk up to Central Park and head to the Bethesda Terrace, which offered her favorite view of the grand stone steps leading down to the Bethesda Fountain with its stunning Angel of the Waters statue. That was where she did all her best thinking.

"I'm going fountain checking," I told Tom. "I'll be back in an hour at the latest if I can't find her. You'll wait here for her?"

He assured me he would. And so I went in search of fountains, and there were plenty. I checked the dancing fountains at the Bellagio first, the choreographed waters shooting two hundred feet up in the air to strains of Pavarotti. No Stella. Next I headed to Caesars Palace, and the landmark fountain there, as big as a city block, was so crowded that I could barely weave my way through to look for a slight brunette.

There! In a tank top and yoga pants and flip-flops was a woman with her back to me, leaning against a marble column.

"Stella!" I called out and ran over.

But when she turned around, it was someone else. Someone at least fifty years old with one hell of a body.

I glanced at the notepaper with names and addresses of ten other fountains, compliments of a concierge at the New York-New York. I got to four others before a blister on my left foot sent me limping back to my hotel.

It was almost nine and getting dark—well, as dark as the Las Vegas strip could get—and I had no idea where my sister was.

"She's okay, right?" I asked Tom over dinner. We'd waited until we were so hungry that we couldn't take it, then ordered room service in my room, just in case she came back or called the room before my cell phone.

"She's okay. She's processing. Accepting that she may never find him. It's a lot to take in. The fantasy probably kept a lot of the fear at bay. And now it's hit her. She's on her own with this baby."

He was absolutely right.

14

STELLA CAME BACK JUST AFTER MIDNIGHT. TOM AND I HAD DOZED off on the bed, and when the door opened we both jumped.

"Oh," she said, surprised. "I didn't realize you were here, Tom."

"You didn't get your twenty cell phone voice mails from me?" I asked. She could have picked up just once. She could have called back just to check in with an *I'm alive, don't worry, just need to be alone.*

She shook her head. "I turned off the phone and never turned it back on. I just wanted to think."

Tom squeezed Stella's hand and left for his own room to give us some privacy. When the door clicked shut behind him, she said, "So I guess you made up your mind."

"Do not say another word," I warned her. "He could hear you."

"He *should* hear me. He should know that you're in love with someone else. You owe it to yourself to tell Nick how you feel about him. He came all the way to Nebraska, Ruby! But you can't bear to live without your safety net."

"Well Tom came all the way here," I pointed out. "And he's not a safety net. He's my fiancé and I said yes to him for a reason."

"Because he's safe."

"Because I love him, Stella. You've been telling me I don't for three thousand miles and I haven't agreed with you yet, have I?"

She walked over to the window and stared out at the lights. "I just thought that if I'm going to face reality, you should, too."

"Stella, I don't want to argue with you. You had a really rough couple of days, and it's late and we're both exhausted, so let's just get some sleep. I'm happy to stay here if you need me. But I think we should go home tomorrow. I think that's how we're going to face reality."

She glanced at me, then began reaching into the dresser drawers. She exchanged the tank and yoga pants she was wearing for another set.

"Is that a tattoo?" I asked, eyeing the red heart on her ankle.

"A fake," she said, her voice tight. "So, Ruby, there was another reason I wanted to come out here. The reason I wanted to stop in on Sally Miller along the way."

I stared at her and waited. She didn't say anything. "Stella. What?"

She glanced at me, her big blue eyes up to something. "Daddy lives here."

"*Daddy?* Now he's Daddy?"

"He was the last time we saw him, Ruby. That's what we called him."

She had to be kidding. *Daddy?* "That was over twenty years ago! And didn't we settle this? We talked about Eric Miller way too much on this trip as it is."

"Aren't you curious?" she asked. "Don't you want answers?"

No, I did not want answers. Why would I want anything from that deadbeat thief? He'd walked out on us, all of us, and didn't look back. And not only did he take his "cut," but he'd never paid one penny of child support to our mother. He'd never sent a birthday card. Not a single one. Why—how—had he let our seventh birthday pass without at least sending a card? Just a fake Hallmark greeting to let us know that a) he was alive and b) he was thinking of us, did love us, in his own way. Instead, we got dead air. And check the mailbox, we did. For the week leading up to our seventh birthdays, we opened and closed the little black door to the mailbox at least twenty times a day, asking our mother over and over if she'd taken out the mail, if a card had come for us. We would have been happy with one card addressed to both of us.

The card never arrived. Not leading up to our birthday,

not on our birthday, not belatedly, either. We must have broken our mother's heart with our checking and pleading and constant conversation about it, about how sure Stella was that a card was coming, and how sure I was that elephants would fly first. I hadn't wanted to be right. We did pretty much the same thing, on a slightly lesser scale, on our eighth birthday. On our ninth, only Stella bothered. And she never stopped, until she left for New York. She'd probably been checking her mailbox for a birthday card from Eric Miller all these years.

Why did Eric Miller deserve to know us now?

She walked back over to the windows and leaned against the windowsill. The sheer drapes fluttered with the very necessary air conditioner. "We're here, Ruby. And so is he. He lives here. Grammy Zelda told me."

My mouth dropped at that one. "Grammy Zelda? How does Zelda know where Eric Miller lives?"

"When I told her that we were going to Las Vegas for a vacation—of course I didn't tell her about J or about you possibly getting married there—she said that Mom told her."

"Mom?" I repeated. What?

"Zelda said that Mom started tracking him about ten years ago, just in case we ever wanted to look for him. Mom figured that with what she knew of his background, relatives, job stuff, whatever, she would have an easier time."

"And the last place she tracked him was here?" I said. "Why wouldn't Mom have told us herself?"

"I asked Zelda that, but she didn't know. She thought that maybe Mom just wanted the information left for us, so that if we ever did want to find him, we would have a starting point. Zelda said the information is at least ten years old."

Almost as if she tracked him until we were eighteen and legally adults. "But, Stella, it's not like Mom ever brought up the subject of finding our father to *us*. She didn't say, 'You know, if you ever want to find your father, I can help you with some history on him.'"

"It doesn't mean she would have been against it, Ruby. If she were, why would she bother tracking him down?"

"And why would *we?*" I asked. "What could you possibly want to know after almost twenty-five years?"

"It's about closure," she said. "No, actually that's bullshit. It's about something else."

"What?"

She stared at me, then at her feet. She'd clearly had a pedicure during her solo day. Her toenails were a vampy-red. "*I'm* the one who looks like him, Ruby. Do you know how much that sucks? And what if Silas or Clarissa looks like J? A father he or she will never know. My child will look in the mirror every day and not know who he looks like. I've never been okay with it for me, so how can I make it okay for Silas or Clarissa? I need to get it settled, Ruby."

I nodded. I had no idea how it felt to be the Miller twin who looked like the absent parent, the one who'd left. I looked so much like my mother, took so much comfort in that resemblance, that safety. Our hair was not only practically the same color, but the same texture. And we were blondes with pale-brown eyes, unusual. And all the while, Stella, with her blue eyes and her dark hair and her aquiline nose, looked exactly like Eric Miller.

"Do you know that I once asked Mom if it bothered her that I looked so much like him?"

I took a deep breath. "What did she say?"

"She said she'd been very much in love with Eric Miller and my looking like him just reminded her of how much she liked his looks. She said she was glad I was a constant reminder of the man she'd married and loved so much. She also said she didn't hate him."

I remembered Stella telling me that when we were fifteen, that our mother said she could never hate the father of her children. Stella had been relieved; I'd been confused. Something had been shaken in my permission to hate him.

"If I can find Eric Miller, Ruby, if I can just close that door, I can go home with a better understanding of how to deal with handing my child the same set of circumstances."

"But, Stella, what makes you think you'd be closing the door? You'd be opening a door. Who knows what will happen? What you'll find out."

"I have to be willing," she said. "And I am."

Talk about facing reality.

I knocked on Tom's door, but there was no answer. That was odd. Tom was the lightest sleeper, and he must have known I'd come once Stella and I had talked. I called the front desk to make sure I had the right room.

Turned out there *was* no room anymore. Tom Truby had checked out of the New York–New York ten minutes ago. Which meant he heard what Stella said.

He should know that you're in love with someone else. You owe it to yourself to tell Nick how you feel about him. He came all the way to Nebraska, Ruby! But you can't bear to live without your safety net.

He clearly hadn't heard my response. Like that awful moment in *Wuthering Heights,* when Heathcliff overheard Catherine say terrible things about him, but ran away before he heard her say that she didn't care about any of that, that she loved him like mad, that she *was* Heathcliff.

When had Tom Truby turned into Heathcliff? That was Nick's domain.

In any case, *Wuthering Heights* did not end well, unless you counted in death.

If he was still in the airport, he wasn't answering his cell phone. And if he'd already managed to get on a flight to Portland, I wouldn't be able to get in touch with him for hours and hours.

I sat in the lobby, in all its art deco, golden age of New York splendor, under the lithograph of the Chrysler Building. Not too long ago, Tom had sat in this very club chair. And all was okay with the world. I leaned back and stared up at the ceiling, as impressive as the marble-wonder lobby itself.

I heard clapping and cheers and wolf whistles and sat up straight. A bride and groom were having their pictures taken in front of the "subway station." They were not themers. She wasn't dressed as a mermaid, for example. Last night, while on my mad dash of Las Vegas fountains, I watched the staging of a mer-bride being helped "out of the water" by her groom, a nonfish, while a photographer snapped photos. And then off they went in a white limo. Since arriving in Vegas, I'd seen all kinds of themed couples clearly headed to or from the chapels. There were many Trekkies, too many Elvis and Priscillas (hadn't they divorced back in the 1960s, anyway?), and quite a few anything-goers.

This bride wore a truly beautiful white satin gown, the kind I might like. She looked like a movie star, though being rail-thin and tall probably helped. Her hair was down, but off her face in gentle waves. And her groom, tall, dark, and handsome in his classic tux, was grinning like crazy.

They looked so happy. Happy. They were clearly both where they belonged.

I sighed and leaned my head back down. My cell phone rang, and I lunged for it.

Tom.

"Gun to your head, Ruby. Me or Nick. I don't care about the particulars, I don't want the details, I just want to know. Me or Nick."

I forgot that Tom had been there, that day Nick had said that "gun to his head" was how he made his tough decisions. We'd been in the BLA teachers' lounge, marveling at how the coffee was always terrible, no matter who made it, even Tom, who made great coffee. And then Daniel Parks sat down with a cup of it and chugged it down, and then glanced around for spies, which meant we knew he had some good gossip. He leaned in and told us he had no idea what to do, he'd been offered a better paying job at the regional high school for fifteen thousand more a year. But he didn't like the principal, and he'd been at BLA for six years and could create interesting courses and design curriculum, etcetera, etcetera, which included a crush on a math teacher. What should he do? Take the money or the love?

We all said it was a tough one. And then Nick told us that when he was faced with a choice like that, he pretended someone really violent and merciless was holding a gun to his head and telling him he had to choose now. Or die. What came out of his mouth under those circumstances was the true-blue answer.

"Ruby," Tom said through gritted teeth. "Gun to your head. What's your answer?"

My mind was completely blank. I couldn't conjure up Tom or Nick. The real live men or the miniature head-bobbers. There was just white space where a face, a feeling ought to be.

"Your silence sucks," he said. "When you figure it out let me know." And then he hung up.

15

"RUBY, ARE YOU UNDER THERE?"

I grunted, hoping she'd get the hint and go away, but she yanked the blankets off my head.

"I left for breakfast almost two hours ago and you're still in bed?" she asked, walking over to the windows and drawing open the curtains. Bright one-hundred-degree sunlight flooded the room. It even *looked* hot outside.

I'd been under the covers since I'd gone back to our room last night and could see staying there for a while, all day in fact. "I don't feel well."

Of course I didn't. I'd hurt Tom, who'd stood by me through the thickest of thicks and the thinnest of thins. We'd had our usual share of couple fights, some big, some small, but nothing like this. Nothing that had ever been the potential end.

She came over to the bed and peered at me. "You look okay. You sound okay."

I let out a deep breath. "Tom heard what you said. He checked out of the hotel and flew back. He told me to choose and…"

"And?"

"And I couldn't. He said, 'gun to head, me or Nick,' and nothing came out of my mouth. Even I don't get that."

She stared at me, really stared at me. From every angle.

"Stella, I don't have fifty bucks to spend on hearing that my face registers my misery."

She smiled. "It's on the house." She sat down on the edge of the bed and took my hands as if she channeled spirits, too, and looked me over. "You're definitely miserable. So let me pull a Ruby Miller and break it down for the middle-school crowd. Tom proposed and you said yes. Nick proposed dating, and you said nothing. Now Tom is asking you to choose between him and Nick, between being engaged to him or nothing with Nick, apparently, and at the moment you're choosing nothing. But with no one. Is that a double negative?"

"Not bad," I said. "But why would I choose nothing when I love Tom and want Nick? Why would every fiber of my being come up so dead and blank when asked to choose?"

"We need Dr. Phil," she said. "He'd know."

"Normally if I had a problem or a big decision to make, Tom would tell me I needed space and time. But he didn't give me that."

She took the little coffeemaker decanter into the bathroom to fill it up, then returned and added the packet of grounds to the filter. "I guess he figures you should know if you want to marry him or not."

"I don't know anything anymore."

"So let's have some strong bad coffee and go find our stupid-ass father and see if that tells us anything important about ourselves. It's not like either of us can figure ourselves out on our own. It's not like we have anything else to do, Ruby."

"I don't know, Stella. Last night I was trying to think about looking for our father, and I just don't know."

"Well, I *do*. So therefore, we're doing it. Now get dressed and come with me."

It was nice, someone else taking charge. That it was Stella was slightly scary, though.

We went back to the Internet café with my little spiral notebook and pen. The bad news was that when we typed in *Eric Miller* and *Las Vegas* into the Google search engine, there were 1,950,000 hits. The good news was that when we added the word *agent*, that number shrunk to fifteen hundred.

The really bad news was that there wasn't a talent agency, modeling agency or any agency called The Eric Miller Agency, or some variation.

"Are you two showgirls?"

We turned around to find two aging, balding hippie types with soup bowls of coffee in one hand and pastries in the other.

"Yes," Stella said. "And we're not allowed to speak to tourists."

"Really?" one said. "That seems a little exclusive."

Stella shrugged. "Company policy."

"Our loss," the other said, and the two sauntered toward another female duo spread on the purple sofa.

"I feel a million miles away from that," Stella said, turning back to the computer. "Meeting men, I mean. Being picked up. Flirting. The only action I'll be getting is my belly expanding."

"And I, apparently, will be hanging out with Marco." I froze. "If Tom and I broke up—not that we are breaking up—would I lose Marco, too? I love that dog."

"You'd figure it out. Maybe work out a custody arrangement."

"Tom loves Marco as much as I do. Maybe more." I closed my eyes for a long moment, then opened them. "I don't know how I got here, Stella. One minute I was home in Maine, celebrating my engagement. And the next I'm in some Internet café in Las Vegas looking up our father. What the hell?"

She squeezed my hand. "We're doing the necessary thing. The mother of invention, right? When you don't know what to do, you do the necessary thing. Which is finding

Eric Miller. I know it sounds crazy, Ruby, but I think finding him, meeting him, talking to him is absolutely necessary."

Stella had a way of twisting things so they fit her schemes and plans, but in this case, she was on the money. "Let's just visit as many of these agencies as we can stand," she said. "We'll pretend we're auditioning to be showgirls. Apparently, we pass."

"At almost thirty, we're probably over the hill."

I'd forgotten about our birthdays. July 22. And coming right up. If "take a cross-country road trip in search of your twin sister's baby's father and look for your own, while you're at it," was on some Things To Do Before You're Thirty list, we were on target.

"Do you think our dad even remembers our birthday?" Stella asked. "Thirty is a big milestone."

"Yeah, like thirty years ago, I had two baby daughters, but six years later, I decided I didn't want to be their father, after all, so I just split. I'm sure he doesn't remember the date."

She winced. "When you put it like that, I can see why you're so angry at him."

"I don't know if I'm angry at him," I said. "He's not even like a tangible thing, you know? He's just an idea, really. A former something. There's definitely no *there* there." I took a sip of my coffee, which had gotten cold. "I guess I'm angry at the idea that someone could just walk away from his children. I'd be angry on anyone's behalf."

She nodded. "But you don't want to find out why?"

"I know why, Stella. He didn't care about us. Just like our kind, sweet aunt said. He was a selfish prick and that's all there is to it. That's all there is to him."

"But maybe there's another side to the story," Stella said.

"Like that maybe the casting agent wanted to lock us in a dungeon and in order to save us from that cruel fate, he gave us up?" I suggested.

"I know it sounds stupid."

"Stella, she wasn't our evil stepmother. There was no dungeon."

"I like the fantasy, I guess. It's kept me from really thinking too long and hard about it. About having a father who ran away, who didn't love me." She stared at me. "You like the fantasy, too, Ruby. Maybe that was why you couldn't make a decision between Tom and Nick. You wanted a life with Tom, but you liked the fantasy of Nick. And Nick wanted to turn that fantasy into reality. But fantasy was so much safer."

Whoa. "If fantasy is safer than reality, then it's Nick who's the safety net. Not Tom. Tom is reality. Tom is forever." I shook my head. "No, Stella, this isn't making any sense. How could Nick be a safety net? Aren't I afraid of 'going for it' with him? Aren't I choosing the safer guy, the safer future?"

She twisted her long hair up into a topknot. "I don't know. I just know we're on to something, Ruby. Something really important. For both of us."

I nodded. "I guess we do have to find that asshole."

"If not for that little fantasy of mine," Stella said, "I would have hated Eric Miller like you do, Ruby. And I guess I couldn't stand that."

Did I hate my father? I didn't think I had any feelings for him. I certainly didn't still love him, so how could I hate him? The lack of him all these years, the majority of our childhoods most importantly, was simply a cold, sorry fact.

"Let's just get moving," she said. She eyed the list. "There are five agencies nearish to here. Let's just visit those and see what happens. I doubt we'll find him so fast. But maybe someone at one of the agencies will have heard of him. Maybe the Las Vegas talent world is a small one."

And so Stella and I took a crash course in Vegas transportation, since our flip-flops and sandals weren't exactly serious walking shoes. There was a Las Vegas Boulevard bus, and a double-decker tour bus, and a trolley system, so between them, we should get around okay.

We started with the Miller Talent Group, on the third floor of a nice enough building on a side street just a few blocks off the strip. Several people were sitting in the waiting room, a mix of men and women, of all ages. There were Miller Talent Group brochures on every available surface. They specialized in actors, models, extras, look-alikes, specialty acts, narrators, showgirls, and celebrities for everything including television, film, commercials, print campaigns, conventions, trade shows, sales meetings, and special events.

Stella and I walked up to the reception desk. The receptionist, who reminded me of what an aged-out showgirl must look like, smiled with very white teeth.

"Good morning," I said. "Does an Eric Miller work here?"

"There are three Miller brothers, and none are named Eric," she said. "Would you like to fill out an application?" she added, looking between me and Stella. "You both have lovely smiles and excellent skin."

"Thanks," I said and Stella beamed. A compliment always buoyed her spirits, despite how many she must get all the time.

"Have you heard of an agent named Eric Miller?" Stella asked her. "We're trying to track him down."

"Did he close shop and take off with your picture fees?" she asked.

"Something like that," I said.

She shook her head. "Jerk-offs like that give reputable agents like the Miller brothers a bad name. Sorry, girls, but I don't know any Eric Miller. But I'll tell you, I've been working here for seventeen years on and off, and you two would be booked in a *snap* for regular people jobs. Infomercials, that kinda thing." She must have caught Stella's *Huh? Moi, a mere regular person?* expression because she added, "Don't get me wrong, you're both very attractive, but the competition for the model and actor jobs is fierce. You have a much better shot of getting work as a regular type if you're pretty."

That seemed to make Stella feel better. "Well, it's not like I'm twenty-two anymore," she said as we left, admiring herself in the large oval mirror hanging by the door.

"You mean it's not like we're *two* anymore," I corrected. "That was the last time we were in really high demand." Outside in the hundred-degree-plus heat, I asked Stella what she planned to say to Eric Miller when we found him. *If* we found him.

She wrapped her hair into a high bun and secured it with a Miller Agency pen. "Just hi, for starters. We were in town and heard you lived here, so we figured we'd look you up. How the hell have you been?"

"Is that really what you're going to say?"

She shrugged. "Won't know until I see him."

We went to two more agencies that didn't require public transportation. Same drill. Except the receptionists either didn't think we'd make it as regular people or they just weren't the chatty types. I wondered if this was what our own quick exit from kiddie modeling had been like. Our agent getting constant nos, sending us on "go-sees" and being shot down. I couldn't remember those days at all. Just random snapshots of experiences, a studio here, a makeup chair there (yes, at three years old, full makeup).

We walked along the strip and bought ice-cold lemonade from an outdoor kiosk, then stopped at the Bellagio fountain to watch the water dance to Frank Sinatra.

Stella absently sang along to "Fly Me to the Moon," pressing the side of the ice-filled plastic cup to her forehead.

"Grammy Zelda always said that if you ever need to find out something, you should go to the biggest yenta. Who would be the equivalent of an old busybody among Las Vegas talent agents?"

"An old-time agent with sad-sack clients who can't get booked," I said. "Kind of like Broadway Danny Rose. But older."

I reached into my purse for my cell phone, got out my list of agents and called the first agency we went to, the one with the chatty receptionist. Apparently, Freddy Jones-Jones was our man. Been around for forty years and knew everyone and everything about the talent biz in Las Vegas.

"If this agent you're looking for ain't dead, then Freddy will know where he is," the woman said.

"Oh, sure, I remember Eric Miller," Freddy Jones-Jones said. "He showed up in Vegas, let me think—" He leaned back in his rickety black leather chair and chewed the inside of his cheek. "Early, no—maybe mideighties. He had that big pouf of hair, I remember that. He modeled himself on Don Johnson from *Miami Vice*. Remember that show? White suits with pastel shirts. He and his wife had their own little agency. Minor talent. Let me think—what was it called?"

As Freddy thought deeply, flipping through his Rolodex and staring up at the ceiling, I glanced around, wondering if Freddy had any clients. The little office was immaculate, not a piece of paper to be seen. Freddy's office was located on the top floor of a five floor walk-up in a dingy building far off the strip. On the walls were signed glossies of men and women that he probably represented in his better days.

"We researched online, but couldn't find any record of him," I said. "Do you know where he works now?"

"Some hole-in-the-wall storefront," he said. "But he doesn't go by that name anymore. Hasn't in years. He and the Mrs. had to close up shop to beat an outstanding arrest warrant from another state. Something about parking tickets. I heard they were living in an RV so they couldn't be tracked. But I know he hung up a shingle with a new name. Changed his own name, too. Well, not legally, of course. Probably started doing everything under the table."

"Do you happen to remember the name of his agency or his new name?" Stella asked, taking a deep breath.

"I'm sure it's in this mess of a Rolodex somewhere," he said, flipping through the cards. "Although you know, you're not really supposed to call it a Rolodex. *Rolodex* is actually the brand name, like Band-Aids."

"And Xerox," I said.

Stella shot me a look that said: Why are you talking about nonsense when the important information of our lives—at that very moment, anyway—was at hand? Or not.

Freddy continued flipping. He stopped on a card, and Stella and I leaned forward, eyes wide. "I have to remember to call this dope," he said, jotting down a name and number. "The weasel owes me twenty-five bucks from fifteen years ago. I should charge him a dollar a day interest."

Stella stared at him. "Eric Miller?"

"Nah, some other guy." The flipping continued. "Ah. Here it is," he said, stopping on a card and tapping it with his fingers. "Yup. Got it. Michael Roberts."

"Michael Roberts?" I repeated. "Are you saying Eric Miller changed his name to Michael Roberts? Why would someone change their name to something so common?"

"For that precise reason," Freddy said. "There are probably tens of thousands of Michael Roberts in Nevada. Cops would never track him down."

A new name. To avoid paying parking tickets, he changed his name. It was a good thing we hadn't tried to find him before. To discover that he'd changed his name, had made himself unfindable, would have been hard to take, hard to understand.

What it clearly meant was that he didn't want to be found, didn't want his children to be able to look him up.

Stella stood and thanked Freddy, who then gave us the "we should sign with him" spiel. But this time, all his compliments didn't do a thing for Stella.

16

WE FOUND HIM. JUST LIKE THAT.

"Michael Roberts" and his wife, Bunny Roberts, owned the Star Quality Talent Agency for, according to their ads and Web site, those with "Star Quality!" The office was located far west of the strip.

The online bio on Michael Roberts indicated that he'd been serving Las Vegas talent for over twenty years and before that was a "hugely successful" talent agent in New York City. There was a picture, and the moment before Stella and I first clicked on the *About The Agents* link, we took deep breaths and said here goes, and there was our father.

Twenty-four years older than the last time we saw him, yet his angular face, the strong nose, the piercing blue eyes, and the thick dark hair—that hadn't changed. He was still handsome in his midfifties, but there was a dated quality to his style, to the hair, a little *too* Sonny Crockett, parted in the middle. A gold bracelet was visible on his wrist.

I had such few memories of him. Despite him chauffeuring us to and from jobs, despite the evening seminars (which he taught in the living room) in manners and charm, in smiling and holding a natural smile for the camera and a go-see, I remembered next to nothing. I'd once told my mother how surprised I was that I had around five memories, and she'd said I'd likely blocked them as I grew up, the heart's way of protecting itself. She'd insisted he was a good father then, that he'd loved us, that he'd been overly focused on our careers, but that he did love us. She had no explanation for his abandonment other than he was a rainbow chaser. It took me years to understand what that meant.

Bunny Roberts I did not remember at all. If she was the same casting agent who'd run away with Eric Miller, I couldn't tell by looking at her photo. She had the aged-out showgirl look about her, too. Hair too long and highlighted and teased, makeup too heavy, smile too obsequious.

"So what do we wear to meet our long-lost father?" Stella asked, looking on her side of the closet and mine, in our drawers. "Teacher clothes?"

"Us clothes," I said. "Us as we are. You in that and me in this."

Which was Stella in the pretty white cotton dress she'd bought from the Double Sisters and me in khaki capris and a white V-necked T-shirt, my mother's small silver hoops in my ears.

"Flip-flops and all," I said, eyeing our feet.

"Do you think he'll recognize us?" she asked, closing the drawer. "When we walk in? Will he stare at us and say, 'Oh my God, *Stella? Ruby?*'"

"We were six a long time ago."

"But we look the same," she said and we glanced at our reflections in the mirror above the dresser. "Sometimes I look at old pictures and I can't believe how little we've changed. We're just adult versions with the same faces."

"I think that goes for every person in the world, Stella."

"I want him to recognize us," she said.

Back to the fantasy. But I wanted him to recognize us, too.

It took us a long time to actually walk in the door. The agency was a third floor walk-up. We stopped on each level, mild panic attack nipping at both of us.

"Let's run in there first," I said, gesturing at the Alison Gold, Acupuncturist sign on the door at the end of the hall.

Stella grimaced. "I don't think having needles stuck in my head would make me less stressed and nervous right now."

Grammy Zelda swore by acupuncture. I'd tried it once, just to experience it, and it was very relaxing. You really didn't feel the needles. I stood there, trying to stay with the memory of lying on a table, needles protruding from most of my body's surfaces, anything to keep from moving an inch or actually walking up the last flight of stairs.

"Let's just get it over with," Stella said, giving me a nudge forward.

The office was at the top of the stairs. A sign on the glass-paned door read: *The Star Quality Agency.* We squeezed hands one last time, and I waited for Stella to do the honors of pulling open the door, but she just stood there, staring at the doorknob. I joined her in that for a few moments, then grabbed it and twisted.

There were actually a few people in the waiting room. Two women and one man, all reasonably attractive. The three glanced up at us as we came in, then resumed flipping through the magazines or portfolios.

Michael Roberts was nowhere to be seen. Relief.

The waiting room was on the small side, but clean and perfectly presentable, not quite the old, peeling place I'd envisioned, complete with one of those ancient, noisy fans. The walls were painted a lemon-yellow and the chairs were a light wood. At the entrance was a table with brochures for the agency and copies of a pamphlet titled *How To Make It In Las Vegas.* Number one on that list was Believe in Yourself. There was also a bowl of wrapped mints. Stella grabbed one and held it in her palm, but didn't unwrap it.

I could see the T-shirt (or in Stella's case, tank top) now: I Went To Vegas To Find My Father And All I Got Was This Stupid Mint.

It was Bunny Roberts at the reception desk. She looked

exactly the same live as she did in the glamour shot. Her hair was frosted, and she wore too much makeup, but I could see she was pretty. She flashed a lot of deep cleavage. She wore a peach suit in a stretchy fabric that was actually stylish, with a low-cut, ruffle-rimmed camisole underneath. I could imagine her in a convertible Cadillac with a silk scarf wrapped around her head.

"Welcome," she said with a smoker's rasp and a warm smile. She handed us each a clipboard with a long double-sided questionnaire. Application for Representation, it was titled.

Stella and I glanced at each other, then took the clipboards with their little spiral-attached pens, and sat down in the chairs that faced the door behind Bunny's desk. The one with the plaque that read: Michael Roberts, Executive Talent Agent.

I stared at the door. I doubted he would personally usher in his next potential clients. But perhaps when someone came out of his office, he would survey the room, see us sitting there and stop dead in his tracks with the *Stella? Ruby?*

The door opened and a Whoopie Goldberg look-alike emerged. Michael Roberts was behind her. Whoopie turned and said thank you again for meeting with her, and again, she was open to home parties, and Michael Roberts responded with a very original "I'll be in touch."

And then he glanced, for just a split second, at those waiting to meet with him, including the two daughters he hadn't seen in twenty-four years, and without a flicker of recognition, walked back in his office and shut the door.

"Well," Stella said, turning to look at me. "Well."

"Well," I said.

I took Stella's hand and stood. Stella did, too. We glanced at each other, then walked to Bunny's desk. Stella stared at her flip-flops.

"My name is Ruby Miller, and this is my twin sister, Stella. We'd like to see our father."

Bunny's mouth dropped open. The smile returned, then faltered, then returned, then she shot up and darted into the office behind her.

We held our breaths and waited. And waited.

A few minutes later, Bunny came out. "Mr. Ro—I mean, he'll see you now."

My hand froze on the doorknob. Stella opened it and we walked in. The Man Formerly Known As Our Father was standing in front of the window, his back to us. He was scared, I realized.

Stella shut the door behind us, and he turned around, neither smiling nor not, exactly. He wore a pin-striped suit with a pale-pink shirt underneath and a white tie. His hair was shellacked in place by hairspray.

"You're both so beautiful," he said in a voice that didn't sound familiar.

Stella and I both had the same awkward almost-smiles on our faces. It was so dead silent in the room that we could hear the hum of the air conditioner. I supposed you couldn't just have a normal conversation after twenty-four years of nothing.

"We thought it was important to find you," Stella said. "Find out once and for all why you left."

He didn't move from the window. His own awkward smile came and went like Bunny's had. "Well, I…I don't really know what to say. I was a different person then." His voice seemed to be cracking, but I couldn't be sure. Maybe he always sounded that way.

"Do you remember us?" I asked. "Do you know who we are?"

"Of course I do," he said. "Ruby and Stella." He smiled and walked toward us, stopping in front of his desk. "In your day, you were something." His chest puffed up some, as if with pride.

"We just really want to know why you left," Stella said, crossing her arms over her chest.

The puff deflated. "I was never much of a family person," he said, glancing from Stella to me, then to the floor. "I tried for a while, and I got real wrapped up in managing your careers. So much so that I didn't even feel like a father—I felt like a superstar agent."

"So when the jobs stopped coming in, you started feeling more like a father again?" I asked.

"Something like that, I suppose," he said.

"But didn't you love your own children?" Stella asked.

He didn't say anything for a moment. "Something's always been kind of off about me in that regard. I don't mean about you two girls necessarily. I mean in general. Like a cut-off feeling, you know?"

It was a pretty good explanation. And it almost helped. It wasn't so much that he hadn't loved us, but that he *couldn't*. At least Aunt Sally had prepared us for that.

"How's your mother?" he asked.

"Dead," Stella responded.

His lips tightened. "I'm real sorry to hear that."

Stella glanced at me. "Well," she said.

Well.

"I'm glad you girls stopped by," he said, moving back over to the window. "I have thought about you over the years. It was nice to see you again."

Talk about cut off. I supposed there were psychological diagnoses for Eric Miller, but I didn't know what they were.

"We'll show ourselves out," I said.

"Bye now," was his response, and I knew we'd never lay eyes on Eric Miller-Michael Roberts again.

Stella and I walked down Las Vegas Boulevard, both of us quiet. It had taken three buses to get from the Star Quality Talent Agency back to the strip. We would have gladly ridden a fourth just for the blast of air-conditioning.

We stopped in front of the Bellagio, but even the dancing fountains, again choreographed to Frank Sinatra, didn't do a thing for our spirits. For the first time since we'd arrived in Las Vegas, the glowing lights and street performances and dancing fountains and constant action didn't, couldn't, attract our attention.

Stella was jostled from behind, and would usually scream

an "Excuse me!" at the offending jabber, but she barely noticed. "I didn't expect that," she finally said.

"I know. The whole thing was surreal."

"I was so sure he'd recognize us, Ruby. How could he not recognize us? I could understand if it had been just one of us in there, but together, Ruby and Stella, the famous Miller twins—how did he not know us?"

"He explained that, I think. He never really 'saw' us at all. He didn't want to be a father, he wanted to be a big deal agent, and managing our careers when we were in demand made being a father tolerable. So I guess Sally was only half-right about us being just money in the bank to him. It wasn't really about the money. It was more about his problems."

"The whole thing is sickening," she said and actually spit on the sidewalk, to the disgust of the woman standing next to her. "Everything he said was sickening."

"I know."

"I hate this," she said. "And I hate that Silas or Clarissa could be standing right next to their father at a red light, waiting to cross Park Avenue, and they won't even know it."

I stared up at the bright-blue cloudless sky. "I don't know which is harder, Stella. Having your father not recognize you after twenty-four years, or not being able to recognize him at all."

She glanced at me and burst into tears. She stood there in the middle of Las Vegas Boulevard and cried and I hugged her and I started to cry, too, though I didn't think I would.

"Mom took good care of us, Stella. She loved us like crazy. With all her might, all her heart and soul. And we're okay. We take after her. Clarissa or Silas will be okay, too."

"I'm not okay," she said, wiping under her eyes. "My own father didn't recognize me, never cared about me and confirmed it. And I'm standing on a street corner pregnant and alone. I have no idea who the father of my baby is."

"First of all, you're not alone. And, yes, you *do* know who he is," I reminded her. "And that's why you don't regret it, right? Aren't those your very own words? Because that night, Stella, you were in love and over the moon for that man, whether you knew him for a half hour or not. You didn't hesitate. You will always know that, and you'll be able to tell your child that you loved his father."

She stopped crying, sucking in deep breaths, and her face brightened. "I know it sounds stupid, but I really did fall in love with him that night. In the first five minutes. I always thought love at first sight was for idiots. And, Ruby, this is really going to sound bad, but I never thought I'd feel that much for anyone after Silas."

"Why does that sound bad?" I asked.

"I didn't think I should feel like that for someone else."

"Ah," I said. "You feel guilty?"

She nodded. "Silas has been gone a long time and I think he would have been happy to know how I felt that night, how J made me feel. I hadn't felt that since Silas."

"I think Silas *does* know, Stella. I think he knows how happy you were that night. And I think he's watching over you now and I think he'll be watching over you for a long time."

She burst into tears again and wrapped her arms around me, and we just stood there for a good long time until the hundred-degree-plus heat sent us running inside a hotel for the air-conditioning. We bought a pack of tissues for Stella, two ice-cold lemonades with extra ice, and sipped while watching a mime performance in the marble lobby.

Stella reached into her little embroidered pink purse, pulled out the Star Quality mint, and chucked it in a trash can.

That night, while Stella read *The Girlfriends' Guide To Pregnancy* in the lobby so she could catch the mime show again, I found my lithograph and sat down to call Tom. I wanted to tell him about Eric Miller and Michael Roberts. I wasn't sure if he'd let me talk, let me ramble on about myself that way, but Tom was my best friend, the person I lived with, and I needed to talk to him.

My cell phone rang just as I was searching my tote bag for it.

Nick McDermott.

"It's been a week and I haven't heard from you," he said, his voice having its usual effect on my body. "So how about this: I'll fly down to Las Vegas, like tonight, and we'll go to one of those crazy chapels and get married. If it works, it works, and if it doesn't, we can say we tried."

Huh? "You mean like get a quickie annulment to go with our quickie ceremony and quickie marriage?"

I expected the "I'm kidding, Ruby" but it didn't come.

"So what do you say, Ms. Miller?"

He was serious? Really serious? Lunch three times a week and the occasional after-school movie and one night in bed, and he was ready to marry me? "Nick, that's very romantic, but—"

"No buts, Ruby. I think I'm in love with you. And I think you're in love with me. But you're engaged to someone else."

I am engaged to my best friend. A man who does make the earth move for me, emotionally and physically. A man who's been there for me through those thick thicks and those thin thins.

A little test. "Nick, did you know that my great-grandmother, Zelda, will likely move in with me in the next year? And her boyfriend, Harold, too. I'm a package deal."

Silence for a second, then he said, "Well, we don't have to live together right away. I mean, when it comes right down to it, Rubes, we really don't know each other at all. We can just take it day by day."

"Take our marriage day by day?"

"Isn't that really the best way to handle everything?" he said.

A few months ago I told Tom that Zelda would probably need to come live with us for good in about six months. The assisted living center was costing her a fortune, and she said she wanted to spend her money more recklessly on fun with Harold and to spoil me and Stella. Tom immediately asked whether she'd be more comfortable in our room or if he should start working on making the guest room more elderly-friendly. That was Tom.

This was Nick. "Besides," he added, "we can't very well make love day and night with Great-Grandma Zelda walking around."

"I suppose not," I said.

"So, I'll meet you at your hotel tomorrow. We'll have a midnight ceremony and come back hitched. That'll be crazy. Crazy enough to actually work."

Somewhere in that gorgeous body of his I think he meant well, that this high-school proposal was coming from his heart. I'd put him off, then he gallantly came to get his girl, then I rebuffed him and hadn't been in touch since. So he was suddenly proposing—a Hollywood marriage of sorts. Without knowing the answers to any of the questions you should ask before marrying.

Just like that, it was gone. The crush I'd had on Nick Noah McDermott for two and a half years was gone. Because Nick had turned the fantasy into reality and the reality was lacking. Tom was the real fantasy. A forever man.

Stella had been right.

I hadn't needed a gun to my head. I'd needed the right question. From the *wrong* guy.

Three times I picked up my cell phone and three times I put it back down. *Call Tom,* I told myself. But this hesitance was new; this *feeling* was new. And the feeling seemed to be…fear. Nerves. Anxiety. A panic attack in the making.

"Ironic that Tom's causing all these butterflies," Stella said over dinner in our room that night. Though it was our last night in Las Vegas, we couldn't bear one more meal out, one more waiter, one more bill. We each lay on our beds, on our stomach, our dinners on trays. The TV was on for once, tuned to VH1, but if the network still aired *Where Are They Now?* it wasn't on today.

I pushed around spinach leaves in my salad. "I'm so afraid to call him, but why?"

"Maybe you're afraid he's going to break up with you," she said. "Tell you it's too late?"

"No way," I said. "This isn't a deal breaker for Tom. God, Stella, even if I told him I slept with Nick, to either get him out of my system or to find out how I felt, I don't think Tom would break up with me. I think he'd let me find my way. If not to him, so be it. If to him, all the better."

"All the better? Why?"

"Because then I'd be choosing him for the right reasons."

Stella took a bite of her herb-encrusted salmon and then cut a piece for me, which meant it was delicious. "So take advantage of the time and space," she said. "When you're ready to call him, you will."

"But I thought it was between him and Nick. And now I've exorcised Nick. He's gone."

And he was. It was as though a sticky clear film had been lifted from my chest. Where I once felt such longing, I now felt bittersweet tenderness. Nick was my friend, had always been just my friend. I had a feeling that relationship would be easy to repair.

Earlier on the phone he'd said he was a romantic and that

he'd rush across the country if I said the word. I had no doubt he would. I had no doubt he'd carry me in his arms to the craziest wedding chapel, too. All on a big romantic high with nothing to back it up, nothing to support it. No questions, no answers.

"It was never between Tom and Nick, Ruby. It was just always about you. And now you need to ask yourself if you really want to marry Tom Truby."

I looked at my ring, my beautiful, twinkling ring, my mother's ring. It looked so right on my finger. But it suddenly felt very tight.

17

IT WAS HARD TO SAY GOODBYE TO THE CAR, BUT NOT SO HARD THAT Stella was willing to drive three thousand miles across country again. We hadn't driven at all in Las Vegas, except to head for the airport. And now we were going home. Well, Stella was going home, and I was tagging along for a day or two. Regardless of what happened with Tom, I would (eventually) be going home to a full house, to a great-grandmother a few miles away, to a job come September, to a life in full swing. Stella would be returning to an empty apartment and the unknown.

The plan was to help her figure out where to put a nursery in her tiny one-bedroom apartment, make a list of what she needed, do some preliminary baby-proofing, and get her started on her new life-to-be as a mother, and a single mother, at that. In a couple of weeks, she'd fly up for our birthdays so that Grammy Zelda could partake (Grammy was especially big on milestones), and then I'd do the traveling for the foreseeable future.

We sat at the gate, flipping through our magazines, *The New Yorker, Portland, Lucky, Vanity Fair,* and *People,* which I could never resist. We had a five-hour flight awaiting us and another half hour to go on these hard orange seats.

A woman with a baby attached to her chest via a Baby Björn asked Stella if the seat next to her was free. Stella moved her pile of magazines, and the woman smiled and thanked her. All we could see of the baby was the tufts of pale fuzz on its head.

Stella stared at the little head. "I'm due in December," she told the woman. "And nervous."

The woman laughed. "I'm still nervous. But it's great," she added, gently rubbing the material at the baby's back. "Everything you hear about motherhood is true, including that it completely changes your life."

"In a good way?" Stella asked.

She nodded. "In the best way." She waved at a man approaching with an infant car seat and two carry-on bags over his shoulder. "There's my husband," she said, standing. "Forget all the crap those books say you have to buy. All a new mother needs is a good husband. Someone to carry the car seat, you know?"

Stella's face fell, but the woman didn't notice; she was already on the people mover with her helpmeet.

"So you'll carry the car seat," I told her, slinging my arm around her shoulder. "I am woman, hear me roar, right?"

"I guess," she said, grabbing the *People* and loudly flipping pages.

"You're going to be a really good mother, Stella."

She closed the magazine and looked at me with Face Reader concentration. "Are you just saying that? I really want to know."

"I'm not just saying that. You are going to be great. You will make Mom proud, Stella."

Tears glistened in her eyes. "It must have been so hard for her. But she did it with twins. And we were no day at the beach. *I* was no day at the beach, I should say."

"Is a day at the beach ever easy? There's parking, then lugging all your stuff, then remembering where you parked, then finding a good spot, then getting sand kicked at you, then listening to kids shriek, and getting stung by a jellyfish, then finding sand in your lunch, then getting sunburned and having to schlep all the way back to the car for the sunscreen, but forgetting the keys and—"

"I get the point," she said with a smile.

"Mom did it, and so many women do it. Yeah, it helps to have someone to carry the car seat or take one of the 3:00 a.m. feedings. But you already have all you need to take good care of your baby."

"All I need? I have nothing on any of the lists in any of the books I read. I don't even know how to change a diaper."

"You have what you need, Stella," I said, squeezing her hand. "Meaning, you've got what it takes."

"Oh," she said, her face brightening, then lighting to full-out beam. "Thank you, Ruby. I hate getting all ushy-gushy, but that means a lot coming from a sancti-sister like you."

"I love a backhanded thanks," I said, swatting her head with *People*.

Her cell phone rang. It was the first time since she'd picked me up in the red convertible.

"Yes, this is Stella Miller," she said. "Yeah, yes, uh-huh, right. What? Omigod, you're kidding me! That's awesome. Yes, I would." She gave her address and then hung up and turned to me, all smiles. "You will never guess who that was."

"Publishers Clearing House Sweepstakes? You've won a million dollars?"

"I wish. It was that baby-faced cop from Iowa. What was the name of that town? Isley? Anyway, my copy of *What To Expect When You're Expecting* turned up in a stolen car and thanks to your inscription, Baby Face remembered us."

"So he's sending it to you?"

"After the trial. It's evidence apparently. He said he might not have bothered sending the book but he thought I might want back the 'very special' bookmark."

I smiled. "Do you?"

"Let's just put it where it belongs, in Mom's hope chest."

"I second that."

"My cosmetics bag and malt balls weren't with the book." She smiled. "Baby Face said, 'See, Mrs. Miller, you can definitely know *what to expect* from the Isley PD. Justice.' He really emphasized the *what to expect*. I'll bet he couldn't wait to make that little joke."

I laughed. "Did he really call you Mrs.?"

She nodded. "It sounded so weird. Me, Mrs. Miller."

"I know. Most of the kids at BLA call me Mrs. Miller. They figure if I'm a grown-up, I must be married."

Our flight was finally called, but as we were neither first class nor requiring extra help, we still had a while to go in the orange seats with our magazines.

"Ruby, if you do marry Tom, are you going to change your name?"

"I don't know. I was always so attached to Miller because it was my only connection to our father. But now holding on to that doesn't seem so important anymore."

She was quiet for a moment. "You know, I've come to like the sounds of Ruby Truby. There is something very rhythmic, very musical about it."

Which meant big sister Stella was giving her blessing.

Every time I flew into New York City, I dreaded the sight of the skyline. It always reminded me of where we'd come from, that once we'd been a family of four. I would think of my mother, a native New Yorker, packing us up and moving us to a strange new land for a fresh start with no associations. I always thought that staying in Maine was honoring my mother's bravery, her choices and decisions. Once, I'd asked her if it bothered her that Stella ran right back to New York the minute she could. She'd said she didn't mind a bit, that losing Silas very likely sent Stella seeking comfort from the place where her family had been intact.

Meanwhile, a stranger named Michael Roberts, living and breathing across the country, was someone I used to call Daddy. As our plane bumped down on the runway at JFK, I thought less of the old and more of the new. New York City was Stella's home, the home of my future niece or nephew. That was my association now.

And she had one tiny piece of it. Stella's Upper West Side apartment was small, around four hundred square feet. Including the bedroom. It wasn't a luxury building with a doorman, but it did have an elevator.

"I suppose even if it didn't," she said, as the doors pinged open in the lobby, "I would still manage fine without the helpful husband since I'm only on the second floor. And one of the great things about living in New York is that supermarkets deliver. The drugstores deliver. And Buy Buy Baby delivers."

She'd painted since I'd last visited. Instead of the usual dingy off-white of rentals, the walls were a soft pale-yellow, the decor an inviting, cozy Morocco-meets-flea market. Under a painting of Stella on a living-room wall was a pretty white wooden cradle with a tiny white quilt inside.

"I found it at a flea market," she said. "It's fun to wonder what other babies were rocked in it. Maybe Bono's or David Beckham's."

I smiled. "You never know."

"That's for sure," she said.

We spent the rest of the evening on her sofa, making lists. Headers such as What The Baby Needs, which included everything from a crib to diapers, from a nasal aspirator to a baby bathtub. Then there was What Stella Needs, down to the Baby Björn and Lamaze class.

"Can I do Lamaze alone?" she asked, tossing her pad on the coffee table and resting her feet on it. "I think you're supposed to have a partner. But who would be my partner? I have some friends, but not a best friend who'd do that."

"Yes, you do," I said. "Me. I'll be your partner. I'll fly down for the weekly class, and then a couple of weeks before your due date, I'll come stay with you."

She bit her lip, which was often her way to stop herself from crying. "I would really appreciate that, Ruby."

I squeezed her hand. "That's what twin sisters are for."

"Good twin sisters." She let out a sigh and sipped her herbal tea. "God, I'm so jealous of you."

"Me? You're jealous of me? What the hell for?"

"You've just got it so together. Including Tom, Ruby. I realize now that I had that wrong. I mean, I've always gone for Nick types, you know? The bad boy. The unattainable who I had to prove to myself and everyone I could get. But no one can really ever get that guy."

I nodded. "I think you're right about that. Nick proposed, but proposed what? Basically a divorce!"

She laughed. "Yeah. And Tom proposed forever. A life.

A family. A future. The whole shebang, white picket fence and all. And you've never been afraid to say yes to that. To want it. To think you can really have that kind of life."

"You always said that life was a bore," I pointed out.

"Yeah, it's really boring to come home to someone who loves you. To someone you can trust. To someone who cares if you're late or sick or need help with something." I could see tears in her eyes. "I've been such an idiot, Ruby. I've totally had it wrong. You were right before, Tom wasn't the safety net at all. *Nick* was. Because Nick *was* total fantasy. From start to finish. And it's easy to love a fantasy, right? Desiring only the unattainable can keep a person pretty busy. And unattainable herself."

I stared at my sister, this insightful creature who only a few weeks ago seemed like a *Star Trek* alien to me. She was right. Absolutely right.

"And as long as you were in love with Nick," she said, as though thinking out loud, "you couldn't really love Tom, couldn't really commit fully to him. That kept Tom at arm's length. Safe. Am I on target?"

"Bull's-eye," I said, pretty darn impressed. "How did you get to be so smart, anyway? I'm the one who went to the Ivy League college."

She smiled. "School of life, babe. I've been using men and one-night stands as safety nets since Silas. I just didn't really connect the dots."

I knew all about not connecting the dots.

★ ★ ★

Stella had been getting a pillow and a blanket for me for the past twenty minutes. "Stella?" I went into the bedroom, and she was passed out cold on her bed, her head at the footboard.

The radiator cover across from her bed was lined with photographs, Stella and me, Stella and our mother, Stella and me and our mother. And Stella and Silas, arm in arm, at the beach. Soon there would be one of Stella and a baby named Silas or Clarissa.

Earlier that evening, when we'd been in the bedroom with a measuring tape to figure out where the crib would fit best, I'd noticed a photograph I'd seen many times before, of the Miller family at the beach, me on my mother's shoulders, and Stella up on our father's shoulders, all of us squinting and smiling.

That photograph was now gone. I liked that she'd rearranged the others to fill up its place instead of leaving the hole. That told me she was well aware that a new photograph of a new family couldn't and wouldn't be a replacement for what was lost, what had been, but was a testament to life going on, moving forward, ever changing.

Since Stella was lying on top of her comforter, I went into her closet and found the spare blanket and draped it over her, then shut the light and closed the door. In the living room, I lay down on the sofa, putting a square pillow under my head and spreading out the chenille throw on top of me. I reached for my cell phone and pressed in Tom's number.

"I miss you," he said. "And I'm really, really, really angry at you."

"I know. And I have a lot to tell you, a lot to apologize for. But right now I want you to know that I've figured out some very important *stuff,* for lack of a better word. Stuff I didn't even know *was* stuff."

"I've always known you have stuff, Ruby. It's one of the reasons I thought going off into the wilderness with Stella was such a good idea."

"And it was. Want to know what I figured out?"

"Yup," he said, and it was as though he were right there in the room, snuggled with me on the couch, his warm, intelligent blue eyes intent on me.

"I figured out that it's always been you, Tom, right from the get-go. From day one at BLA. I thought I had some kind of big crush on Nick, but it turned out I was just using that crush to keep you at enough of an internal distance. To protect myself, just in case. Just in case you left."

"I'm not going anywhere," he said.

"I believe that now. I trust in that. I guess I never really did before."

"So I guess you'll have to let down the BLA heartbreaker. That might be a first."

"Actually, I already did. But you know what? I'll bet it's not the first time."

"Probably not," Tom said.

I suddenly knew that it was true. That Nick had been hurt before, somewhere along the way, and he wasn't ready to free fall. He'd come close with me, he'd taken a step. And when the right woman crossed paths with him, he'd be ready to give her all of himself. She'd be one lucky woman.

18

The next morning, Stella and I took the subway to Buy Buy Baby, a huge baby emporium. There were aisles upon aisles of everything you never thought of, despite having read all the books and scanning all the checklists, such as sunshades for the rear passenger windows and a warmer for diaper wipes.

Stella walked in with no idea of what she wanted the nursery to look like. Yet with the hundreds of cribs to choose from, simple or ornate, she fell in love with a white Jenny Lind crib with its spindles and old-fashioned charm. It was a perfect match for the cradle. She chose soft, pale-yellow sheets and a matching crib bumper with sunwashed blue cartons of blueberries. Armed with our lists, we knew what we were looking for. Into our carts went the Diaper Genie, the wipes, and newborn-size Pampers, the wipes warmer, just because, and several onesies and sleepers in all different colors. We'd researched the infant car seat and stroller beforehand, so that made choosing those easy. Stella went for a white Jenny Lind changing table and a thick terry-covered mat. All the heavy stuff would be delivered to her apartment.

There were aisles upon aisles of so much stuff that Stella said she couldn't possibly spend another half hour choosing between nasal aspirators and tiny nail clippers. She had months to round out the nursery and her medicine cabinets. As we neared the checkout, two overflowing carts between us, she added an adorable clock with an illustration of the cow jumping over the moon and a matching night-light.

I insisted on paying for everything. Despite Stella's stash—it turned out that she had taken good care of the money she'd inherited from our mother—I wanted to treat her, wanted to be the doting relative who showered her with what she needed, what the baby needed. She argued and shook her head and tried to elbow my credit card out of the way with her own, but then finally relented with a hug.

Outside, as we spent at least twenty minutes trying to hail a cab, the hot, humid New York City air reminded me of how much I missed the cool bay breeze in Blueberry Hills, the ocean at the ready just minutes away. In just a few hours, I'd be heading to LaGuardia Airport and boarding a plane bound for home, home to Maine, home to Tom, home to being Ruby Truby. To being me. Without hesitation and without a safety net. Safety nets were what friends were for. And sisters.

For our last meal together on our cross-country extravaganza, we both wanted good New York Chinese. Stella's favorite restaurant was a fifteen-block walk south (an issue only because it was so hot and sticky out), but there was a street fair along a stretch of Amsterdam Avenue, which meant funnel cake for dessert on the way back.

A blast of air-conditioning greeted us at Lucky Duck. We were seated by the front window, the curved, dark red *Lucky Duck* letters backward above our heads. Stella had brought her camera to photograph the big furniture items at Buy Buy Baby so she could mentally decorate her apartment before delivery, so I asked the waiter if he would go outside and take a picture of us, making sure to get the sign in the photo. I felt guilty sending him out into that heat, but he happily went, snapping two just in case.

We were debating between sesame chicken or chicken in garlic sauce when someone called Stella's name. We both glanced up to find a very good-looking guy smiling at Stella. She gasped, both hands flying to her face.

"I'm not sure if you remember me, but—" his cheeks pinkened a bit "—we met a few months ago…in the bar at Georgina's?"

My mouth dropped open.

"Jake," she said.

He nodded.

She was barely able to contain her burst of smile. "I've been looking for you."

He was all smiles, too. And he did bear a striking resemblance to Hugh Jackman, brown eyes and all. "I've been looking for you, too. I went back to Georgina's a bunch of times, but never saw you. And I couldn't remember the other places we went or where you lived."

He was ridiculously cute. Tall, about six-feet-one, and lanky, but broad-shouldered. With one dimple. His brown eyes were so open and honest. He had dark-brown hair, thick and wavy.

"Jake, the night we met, did you say something about Las Vegas?" Stella asked.

He nodded. "My brother had his bachelor party there. We stayed an entire week at Caesars."

Stella and I almost fell off our chairs. "You were in Las Vegas for an entire week? *Last week?*"

"No, a few months ago," he said. "I left the day after we met." The waiter came by with a chair, gesturing at Jake. "Could I join you?" he asked us both.

Stella was too beside herself to speak.

"Please do," I said, wondering if the baby would get Jake's brown eyes or Stella's blues. The kid couldn't lose.

It turned out that Jake had been passing by Lucky Duck, heading for his health club around the corner, when he noticed Stella in the window. He'd thought the heat and humidity had affected his brain, that his eyes had to be playing tricks on him, that the woman sitting right there in the window couldn't possibly be his dream woman (that was a direct quote), the one he'd spent the past three months looking for.

If we'd been sitting in any other seat, if Stella had gone to the ladies' room just two minutes later, he would have missed her entirely.

Lucky Duck indeed.

Over two chicken dishes, one beef, two kinds of dumplings, and vegetable fried rice, we learned that Jake Singer was a corporate attorney, lived five blocks away, and this was his favorite Chinese restaurant as well.

Stella Singer. Now *that* was musical.

It finally occurred to me that I was crashing their second date. And I needed to take off for home.

I called Stella's cell phone from the plane, which added another gazillion dollars to the cost of the trip.

"I won't even ask questions," I said. "Just tell me everything, in any order!"

She laughed. "Well, after Lucky Duck, he asked if I wanted to go for a walk, and at first I thought we could just stroll through the street fair, but then I realized that a street fair wasn't where I wanted to tell Clarissa or Silas's father about him or her. So, I suggested we walk to Central Park, and I told him at my favorite spot."

The Angel of the Waters statue at the Bethesda Fountain. Where she did all her hard wishing.

"So you did tell him?" I asked.

"I did."

I waited, but she was prolonging the suspense.

"Ruby, I told him—I just came out and told him everything, starting with meeting him, and how I felt, and then not being able to find him, and then driving up to Maine and asking you to drive cross-country with me to find him."

"And he said?"

"He said *wow* a few times. And then he said the news was a little easier to process now that we'd had three dates, if we counted the first meeting, and then Lucky Duck and now Central Park, and that no matter what, he would not disappear on me ever again."

"He said that?"

"He did. Twice."

"When are you going to see him again?" I asked.

"He's coming over in an hour. He's cooking. And bringing the groceries. Apparently, he's quite a chef. Cousin Rory would be proud."

"I'm very glad, Stella. Very, very glad."

"Me, too," she whispered. "What's that saying about how sometimes you have to travel a gazillion miles to find what was right in your own backyard the whole time? Guess we proved that right."

"We sure did," I said. "So what are you going to wear?"

"My Nebraska dress. It has history."

I laughed. "Yes, it does. Bye, Stella. Call me tomorrow?" She promised she would.

Tom was waiting for me at the gate. He had a bunch of orange irises in one hand and the other over his heart. Then he ran over and picked me up and spun us around for a long, hot kiss that definitely made the earth move.

Epilogue

September

PINK BRIDESMAIDS: CHECK. FANCY SEASIDE INN: CHECK.

My wedding planners, aka my soon-to-be sisters-in-law, came over often with thick, glossy magazines and color charts and color samples. Did I know there were seventy-two shades of pink? Did I like taffeta as much as Anne did? Did I know Caroline never liked *peau de soie?* After they devoted an entire week to the "bridal party dress concept," I tuned them out when they turned to shoes. There were hundreds more bullet points to consider (they, too, were armed with checklists), from the wedding gown to the food to the band to the flowers, and I'd much rather plan the upcoming semester than the nuptials.

Caroline and Anne, with their headbands and twin sets,

would only err on the side of dull for the wedding, so they seemed like safe bets. (And a safety net for a wedding was not only okay, it was a good idea.) They were thrilled when I told them I would leave the entire affair up to their good taste, down to the music, as long as "Fly Me to the Moon" was in there somewhere. Tom and I had yet to pick a wedding song, but Frank belonged to me and Stella.

Stella was going to be my maid of honor. Caroline, Anne, and my old friend Amy, my bridesmaids. My great-grand-mother, Zelda, would walk me down the aisle and give me away (oh, how tickled she was by the request!). And Tom Truby would be waiting for me at the end of the aisle.

I had seen Nick only once. I'd called him a few days after returning home and asked if we could see each other in person. He'd welcomed me to his apartment, the bachelor pad that had once been the secret site of all my fantasies and now did absolutely nothing for me.

He was still Nick, still so utterly breathtaking, but my heart was fully elsewhere.

"Our friendship means so much to me," I told him. "It has for the past almost three years. I know that sounds so platitudey and hokey, but it's true. We don't have to lose the friendship, do we?"

"Like you could get rid of me?" he asked. "Not that you didn't do some damage, Ruby. But, I don't know. You were probably right, about me wanting what I can't have, roman-ticizing what's between us. Everything you said on the phone when I called you in Vegas rang true. Hard to hear, but it rang true."

"You're one of my favorite people, Nick."

"Good, because you're still my best friend. I might always wonder about the what-if, but I know you're with the right guy."

Me, too. Except the part about wondering about the what-if. That was over.

Within a month, Nick had moved onto his next conquest, a toughie: the wonderful English chair, Meg Fitzmaurice, who'd warned me away from him on my first day at BLA. She'd taken her own advice for four years, but fell during a weak moment when her husband left her for a younger woman. She *said* Nick was a delicious distraction, but I sensed something in both of them when they were together, something deeper, something growing. Something good.

As for Jake and Stella, they were quite the couple. He'd fallen hard for her, and though they were nervous wrecks about the baby, about being parents while getting to know each other, they were committed.

She called while I was out on the swing with Tom, enjoying the last summer weekend before school started on Tuesday.

"He's so wonderful," she said. "Last weekend he painted a little mural on the wall above Clarissa's crib. To match that adorable clock we found, the cow jumping over the moon. I can't wait till you see it, and see the room now—"

"*Clarissa's* crib?" I asked. "Not Clarissa's or Silas's?"

She laughed. "The whole reason I called was to tell you that it's definitely a girl, but of course my mind is on fifty different things. You should see me, Ruby, I'm as big as a house.

Ginormous. Did you know that word is in the dictionary now? Oh, Ruby, I have to go—the Singers are here. Jake's parents. We're meeting for the first time! They live in Florida. We've only spoken on the phone, and they seem so nice, but of course I'm still nervous. Just think—they're going to be Clarissa's grandparents! I'm so glad she gets grandparents. And an aunt like you. Ooh, gotta go. Love to Tom. Bye!"

It was good to hear Stella so happy. She and Jake were already talking about marriage. Via the *New York Times* Web site, Stella had found and printed out the marriage article, with the questions every couple should ask before marrying, and they agreed they should marry when they both were comfortable answering those questions in the first place.

They had some time to go on that. In the meantime, they would focus on being the best possible parents to Clarissa. (It turned out that Jake loved both names, even when Stella had explained who Silas would be named for.)

Tom returned from the house with a fresh pitcher of lemonade and one of those little battery-operated handheld fans that his nieces had left last weekend. Tomorrow we would put back on our teacher clothes and wake at the crack of dawn and spend our days with tweens and teens. He refilled my glass and we toasted to the last days of summer. Then we linked arms and swung, Tom chivalrously aiming the little fan on me, both of us secure in the knowledge that our answer to question fifteen—the one about whether or not our relationship was strong enough to withstand challenges—was yes.

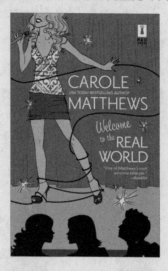

A Rachel Benjamin Mystery

Jennifer Sturman

Rachel Benjamin's weekend of meeting her future in-laws turns out to be quite challenging when she discovers her friend Hilary is missing. As someone orchestrates an elaborate scavenger hunt across San Francisco, dangling Hilary as the prize, Rachel must track down her friend while proving to her future in-laws and her fiancé how normal she really is!

The Hunt

"Sex and the City meets Agatha Christie!"
—Meg Cabot, author of *The Princess Diaries*

Available wherever trade paperback books are sold!

RED DRESS INK
™

www.RedDressInk.com

RDI570TR